BAY
OF
DREAMS

Bay of Dreams

Published by The Conrad Press in the United Kingdom 2019

Tel: +44(0)1227 472 874
www.theconradpress.com
info@theconradpress.com

ISBN 978-1-911546-48-1

Typesetting and Cover Design by:
Charlotte Mouncey, www.bookstyle.co.uk

The Conrad Press logo was designed by Maria Priestley.

Printed and bound in Great Britain
by Clays Ltd, Elcograf S.p.A.

BAY OF DREAMS

NED REARDON

By the same author
Blackberry Bill (The Conrad Press, 2018)

There is a Facebook Page available for *Blackberry Bill*
that contains further information

For Judy

Prologue

*A*lone and afraid in this foreign land, he heads through the darkness along the forest trail towards the burning light. He has neither torch nor weapon, but he knows he is almost at his destination for the smell of smoke is getting stronger and the glow beyond the trees is intensifying and the echoes and droning of their malignant tongues has become that much louder.

Determinedly he pursues his sole purpose; to discover the truth. He must know the truth! Beneath the moonless sky he continues almost blindly but doggedly along the narrow dirt track, buffeted either side by mist and thicket, until he eventually reaches the edge of the clearing. Here, under the keen eye of the old owl above, he halts and conceals himself among the luscious ferns, the hairs lifting on the nape of his neck as he settles down and observes with a morbid interest the drama unfolding before him.

Suddenly the ungodly chanting ceases, leaving a vacuum of blood-curdling silence ubiquitous in the open space. He has counted a dozen figures robed in dark hooded cloaks standing perfectly still with their heads bowed respectfully, forming a perfect crown around the bonfire.

'Devil worshippers!' he utters under his breath, nodding slowly as though affirming his own suspicions. Already he has gained a sense of the incisive bloodlust prevalent among the group, each of them quivering with perverse excitement as the thirteenth member of the cult unemotionally slaughters the sacrificial beast. Presiding over the ceremony and contrastingly adorned in a long, flowing white cassock, their leader holds aloft the blood-drenched carcass and starts to shout out resoundingly into the stillness of the night. The verses he recites are of an ancient, foreign dialect and reverberate terrifyingly in the cold night air.

Linking up and holding hands, the rest of the congregation form a tight ring around the dying flames and proceed to stomp around the circle as though performing a war dance, resuming their satanic chants whilst their principal attempts to conjure up their all-powerful master.

The evil one finally materialises before his loyal followers, who respectfully drop to their knees with gasps of praise, bowing with veneration before his unholy presence. The Devil slowly steps out of the hot, smoking ashes ready to acknowledge his summoner and to survey his newly acquired kingdom.

The young man's skin rapidly turns chilly and he is shivering nervously, for never have his eyes seen something so monstrously grotesque, an abomination that defies belief with curled horns protruding from its head, tomato-red burly flesh, cleft hooves and a huge, muscular tail hanging limp in its crude shadow.

The hideous creature turns round unexpectedly and points directly and accusingly at the person quaking in fear just beyond the dark trees. But the frightened young man has already accepted his fate and has clearly understood that he *must quickly put an end to his own mortality, for he has noticed with the most horrendous disgust that the Devil's facial features are not that of Satan's but are his own instead.*

The hitchhiker woke up gasping for breath and with his heart thumping in distress. Sweating profusely and with his eyes wide open with shock, he screamed out at the car's dazzling lights rushing towards him, *'No, No, No!'*

'You're all right, lad, you're safe!' the hitchhiker heard the lorry driver exclaim. 'You were having a bad dream, that's all.'

'Where are we?' the hitchhiker asked, frantically, vigorously rubbing his eyes.

'Not far from Calais now,' the lorry driver replied. 'You'll soon be home, lad.'

1

A QUARTER OF A CENTURY LATER...

About half a minute after midday, the church bells in Cassone, a serene and sleepy Italian hamlet set on the picturesque north-east flank of Lake Garda, finished chiming.

'Wake up, Grace,' Ralph Ashton said, gently prodding his wife.

Grace was lying sprawled out on a sun lounger in a black swimming costume, her face and limbs coated in a delicate layer of tanning oil. She awoke rather disgruntled.

'What is it, Ralph?'

'You're never going to believe this.'

'Oh, let me sleep, love. I'm tired!' she complained.

'No, wake up darling, you don't understand,' he persisted, excitedly. 'I'm not messing around. This is unreal.'

'What! What do you mean, not real? What are you talking about, Ralph?'

'Look, just sit up and listen for a moment, will you!'

His wife blonde, beautiful, and in her mid-forties, finally

13

succumbed to his demands and reluctantly adjusted her lounger into the upright chair position. 'So, what's so important then?' she demanded. On the small table aside of her was a bottle of local red wine - half full - and two empty wine glasses, an expensive bottle of suntan lotion and a copy of the previous day's *Daily Express*.

'Well, like I've already said love, you're never going to believe me, but I think I've just witnessed a suicide.'

'What!' she exclaimed, craning her head about in every direction, expecting to see a corpse lying on the ground somewhere nearby.

'Grace darling, stop saying *what* and just listen to me for a minute. Look, can you see that house over there, across the bay? The large yellow building at the top of that rocky ledge above the village, the villa set in its own olive grove. Do you see it?'

Ralph and Grace got up from their sun loungers and went to lean against the terrace railings gazing out across the glistening, turquoise waters of the bay. There was a pleasant warm breeze and above them, except for the odd twist of streaky cloud, was an unfurled sky of the brightest blue. They were staring at a cluster of magnolia and yellow dwellings with terracotta roof tiles that were all huddled tightly together on the hillside, as though each were desperately afraid of becoming dislodged from the remainder and plunging into the abyss beneath the water.

This was Cassone. The view of the bay from here was panoramic and the same calm and tranquil scene which Ralph had much admired some twenty-five years earlier. It was also the place where that unbelievably dreadful thing had happened, and his blood suddenly ran cold at the thought of it; something he'd also neglected to tell his wife about and a dark chapter of his life which he thought was best left forgotten.

Grace put on her sun glasses, 'Oh yes, I can see it now.'

Ralph glanced at his watch. It was almost a quarter past twelve. 'I know this must sound absolutely crazy love but less than ten minutes ago I saw a man fall from the top of that building. The poor bloke's probably lying dead somewhere over there in that grove.'

His wife looked at him a tad suspiciously (Ralph had been known to play the odd joke or two) then also down at his empty wine glass, but she knew him well enough to be able to tell when he was sincere and genuinely worried.

'How do you know it was a man, Ralph? Wouldn't it be difficult to tell from here?' she asked sardonically, still squinting behind her dark lenses through the glare of the sun.

'No, it was definitely a man, I could tell by the shape of him. And besides, the guy was nude.'

His wife flashed him a look of surprise. 'What, do you mean completely naked?'

'As the day he was born, Grace.'

Grace frowned and tutted with an air of moral righteousness about her before she asked, almost whispering, 'What was he doing?'

'Nothing really, apart from just standing there, bold as brass, wearing nothing but his birthday suit and peering over the top of the roof.'

After a moment of reflection Grace then said, 'You said you thought it was suicide. Did he jump off the roof intentionally then?'

'Well, not exactly.'

'What do you mean, not exactly?' she echoed, now

worrying a touch herself about the fallen man's wellbeing. 'Either he jumped, or he didn't!'

'Curiously enough, he just kind of let himself topple over the edge. I think he'd been waiting for the church bells to stop ringing, and then over he went.'

Following another brief pause his wife then suggested fretfully, 'Ralph, we've got to tell somebody about this. Maybe we should report it to the hotel manager.'

'Yes, I was just thinking that too. I'll shoot over to the reception desk,' he agreed, pulling on his t-shirt. 'I'm sure they'll telephone the police or somebody. Wait here for me love, I won't be long.'

2

Grace covered herself with a towel and poured herself a second glass of Chiaretto. She gazed back over at the grand old house perched high up on the hillside, her skin goose-pimpled as she tried to picture the scenario her husband had described. It had been Grace who had chosen and arranged this holiday. Not since their honeymoon (an overcast week on the Costa del Sol) almost twenty years ago, had they been able to travel abroad. They simply hadn't been able to afford it and had gradually become resigned to holidaying at seaside resorts nearer to home, in Devon, Cornwall and Norfolk, although they'd visited Wales once or twice and had even ventured as far up as the highlands. But now, at least as far as she was concerned, their boat had finally come in.

No more breaks in Britain ruined by the inclement weather. From now on it would all be sun, sea, and sangria, and why not? Grace thought. Through sheer hard work and an unassailable tenacity to get on in life (Ralph as a structural engineer and herself as a part time, self-employed gardener) the Ashton family had finally made it. At last they were well off, comfortable as some might say, their mortgage redeemed on their three-bedroomed property located on the banks of the River Medway in Rochester, Kent and their kids formally educated; Melissa just married and expecting her first baby in the spring and Geoffrey soon to begin a career in teaching.

They now had sufficient funds set aside for this and that and for a rainy day too, not to mention the sizeable pension pot they'd also accumulated over the years to be spent and enjoyed in the not too distant future. And now, for once in her life, Grace intended to concentrate on herself. Since the beginning of the year she'd remained adamant that their next vacation would be overseas, preferably somewhere in Europe, finally settling on this much renowned Italian beauty spot.

Thinking back though, for some strange reason unbeknown to her, her husband had become noticeably nervous at the thought of spending his fortnight's holiday in Italy. At the time she'd thought it very odd, but could only assume that this was probably due to his past resistance to the idea of travelling farther afield or maybe it was just his fear of flying. Nevertheless, she had eventually got her own way.

A little more than twenty minutes later, Ralph returned with the worried-looking manager. There followed a frenzied period of fuss and excitement among some of the other hotel workers, who had one by one joined the Ashtons out on the sun terrace. They were all busy chatting and pointing, scanning the hilltops across the bay for any further evidence of the fallen man. Several other holidaymakers had also swollen the party of onlookers, many secretly greatly enjoying the unexpected excitement.

Suddenly the manager's mobile phone rang, emitting a loud and silly ringtone. He answered it and briefly said something in Italian before quickly hanging up again. Then he clapped his hands together signifying the end of everyone's amusement. Apparently the police, the local police, had just pulled up into the hotel's car park, so the manager further requested that the English couple should now please accompany him to the reception area. The staff dispersed unwillingly, just as curious as when they'd first arrived, but now they resumed their respective workplace positions.

3

Through the glass façade of the Maximillian Hotel in Val di Sogno, the Ashtons watched, somewhat subdued, as the two plain-clothed policemen got out of the Fiat Saloon police car and entered the foyer. The manager, slightly timorous and waiting just beyond the main entrance, introduced himself first and then his English guests to the policemen.

The older man was the detective inspector in charge, a six-foot, silver-haired, rather distinguished-looking gentleman and ruggedly handsome but to some extent haggard by a long-drawn-out recent divorce. He told them his name was Inspector Allessandro Leopardi. His younger assistant, a dark, curly headed, grievous-looking man, was carrying a set of binoculars in a brown leather case. Both the Italians were dressed smartly in grey suits and spoke relatively good English.

After all the introductory formalities had been dispensed with, the younger man, who had introduced himself as detective sergeant Antonio Bellini, said, in rather good but heavily accented English. 'Well, first would you please show us the place where you saw the man jump.' They'd already been briefed at the police station with outlined details of the incident through the manager's telephone call.

Back on the sun terrace, Ralph duly pointed out the lone villa across the bay above the pretty village. Leopardi focused his binoculars onto the building in question.

'Now then *Signor* Ashton, are you quite certain that's the house?' he asked, affably prompting Ralph to affirm this by offering him the use of their binoculars.

'Yes inspector,' Ralph maintained, taking a long, careful look through the policeman's lenses. 'I'm positive that's the property he fell from, the large yellow mansion house.'

'Ah *si*, I know it,' the inspector claimed, 'The Machiavellis' place.'

On learning this, Ralph felt like his heart had just been pierced by a sliver of ice. He suddenly went weak at the knees.

'Nobody lives there now of course,' the policeman continued, retrieving a mobile phone from his inside pocket. 'The old place has stood empty for many years, almost falling down now, so I'm told.'

Just then the anxious manager returned with a member of his staff in tow, a barman performing a skilful balancing act with a tray of complimentary hot coffees. 'Ah *grazie, grazie,*' said both the policemen.

'*Prego,*' the manager returned amiably, before hurriedly making himself scarce again. He held no desire to be interviewed himself, or to prolong their stay. The presence of the police in his five-star hotel certainly wasn't good for business. Both the Ashtons and the two policemen then sat down at one of the empty tables next to the terrace railings.

Inspector Leopardi had dialled his phone and was waiting for it to answer.

'With respect, inspector,' Ralph complained, 'I don't think *cappuccinos* are appropriate right at this present moment, the man could be lying over there seriously injured or even dead!'

Leopardi splayed out the fingers and thumb of his left hand as a polite gesture to reassure Ralph that all was well before speaking into his mobile phone. Conversing in his own language, he then proceeded to guide his colleagues up through the woodland above Cassone until they'd reached the olive grove situated directly beneath the rocky ledge. 'Please calm down *Signore*,' he said, after he'd finished communicating with his fellow officers. 'We have the matter firmly in hand. Emergency services have already been rushed to the scene and we've got a handful of our best uniform boys searching the area as we speak. Look there, across the lake, you can see the blue lights already.' The sound of the sirens had also begun to resonate across the bay.

Ralph held his tongue while the barman prepared their hot drinks. When he'd finished, Grace carefully passed one of them to her husband who, she noticed, had turned white. 'What's the matter darling? Are you feeling OK, Ralph?'

The policemen both studied Ralph with much evident suspicion as they sipped their coffee, looking at him more closely, then at each other rather discerningly, both wondering why the guy was suddenly acting so strange. They'd noticed how quickly he'd become fidgety and restless.

Ralph shook a disturbing memory away from his mind. 'Er, yes…I'm fine love,' he stuttered. He was now regretting having raised the alarm. I should have kept my big mouth shut, he thought. In hindsight, getting himself roped in with the Italian police wasn't a very smart thing to have done. But it was too late now, so he decided to just play along as the innocent bystander. All he wanted was for them to hurry up and get on with it. The quicker this was over, the better.

'Now sir,' the sergeant began, poised with his notebook and pen. 'Would you mind explaining to us what actually happened?'

'Well, there isn't much to tell really. The guy just simply fell off the building.'

'*Si*, but from the beginning please. Will you describe exactly each detail you can recall? For example, what time was it when you first noticed this man?'

'Just before twelve noon.'

'Are you sure, how do you know this?' the inspector asked.

'Definitely, because within a few minutes of noticing him I heard the church bells start to ring.'

'Ah *si*, please continue.'

'Well we, my wife and I, were both sunbathing, lying down just about there I think,' he said, pointing at a couple of vacant sun loungers. 'Grace was taking a nap and I was just relaxing, enjoying the view over the lake. Then I suddenly noticed this man standing on the roof of that building, completely naked.'

'Umm, *non capisco*,' the inspector interrupted.

'He wasn't wearing any clothes, boss,' his sergeant clarified.

'Did you see this man actually walk up to the boundary of the roof?' the inspector asked.

'No, he was already standing at the edge when I first noticed him.'

'And you believe he was, how you say, completely *nackid?*'

Ralph resisted an urge to smile, having calmed down marginally. 'Yes, inspector, at first I just assumed he was going to lie down somewhere on the roof to sunbathe. But instead he just stood there, balancing dangerously on the rim of the roof, like he'd gone up there on purpose, intending to jump off just as soon as the church bells had ceased.'

'Could you elaborate please, what made you think he was specifically waiting for the sounding of the bells to end?'

Ralph paused for thought. 'I don't know really. I just had this horrible feeling that as soon as everything had gone quiet again, the man was going to kill himself.'

'What happened next?'

'Nothing, he just stayed there swaying precariously, with his arms spread out to the sides.'

'*Scusi, non capisco* please, how do you mean?'

Ralph sprang up out of his chair and proceeded to mimic the suicidal man's actions, stood upright, legs perfectly together, arms held out horizontally and head held high.

'Ah *si*, you mean like a Jesus man?' the inspector suggested.

'Well yes, if you like, just like Jesus Christ on the cross.'

The inspector paused momentarily to take stock of the situation. 'And then when the church bells stopped, he fell yes?'

'Yes, he just kind of let himself tip over the side,' Ralph replied, returning to his seat.

The inspector then asked, 'Did you hear the man make any kind of sound when he fell?'

'No, after the church bells had finally fallen silent everywhere became hushed again, as it usually does. Besides, I doubt very much if we could hear a human voice from over here.'

The inspector shrugged his shoulders, 'Possibly not.'

Sergeant Bellini then asked, 'Tell us, did you notice anything else out of the ordinary when this happened?'

'At the time I could hardly avert my attention away from

the man,' Ralph explained. 'So, no I can't say I noticed anything else.'

'Yes, I see, *Signore*. Lastly then, did you notice anyone else on the rooftop, either before the man fell or after?' the inspector asked.

'No well certainly not before.'

'And what about after he fell?'

Ralph closed his mouth and slowly shook his head before replying, 'No, I didn't see anyone else. But then after I'd pointed it out to my wife, I rushed off to report it to the manager. I can assure you he wasn't pushed, Inspector, if that's what you're implying. Possibly he may have fainted before he'd fallen over, that's my only theory.'

'Yes, and while Ralph was fetching the manager,' Grace interrupted, 'I kept a vigilant watch myself and I never saw anyone else on the roof.'

The inspector's mobile phone bleeped. He answered it and said, 'Leopardi.' Then he listened carefully to the caller's voice. 'OK,' he replied, '*Si, grazie... si... ciao.*' He then addressed his sergeant reverting to English, almost deliberate it would seem, as if he clearly wanted Ralph to understand the meaning of his words. He said, 'You had better contact the town hall, Bellini, we may have to search the Machiavelli estate as well.' The inspector emphasised the latter as if he were attempting to gauge a reaction in the Englishman's manner.

Having made a mental note of Ralph's jitteriness, the inspector said, 'Right then *Signor* Ashton, we're just about done here. Thank you very much for your co-operation. Now I'm afraid, we must get along to Cassone,' he concluded, offering both Ralph, who had gone ominously quiet, and Grace his hand of friendship. 'We'll let you know the outcome of our findings as soon as we can. *Arrivederci, Signor* Ashton.' He then smiled respectfully at Mrs Ashton, '*Signora.*'

Machiavelli. Just through having heard the name spoken out aloud had caused Ralph to feel nauseous and more than a little unsteady on his feet. Had the past finally caught up with him? This is what he'd feared all along. *It's all coming back*, he fretted. *Coming back to haunt me!*

4

The following day's scheduled event was set to be the highlight of their holiday, a day trip to Venice, the city of lovers and a place which Grace had always yearned to visit. But Ralph, who'd been there once before back in his youth, felt completely drained of all his enthusiasm. He supposed he must go, if only for his wife's sake, but all the same he wasn't looking forward to it now.

Feigning a headache, he'd gone for a stroll along the shore to get some fresh air and to do some straight, honest thinking. But as he began to address the concerns that had plagued him since his interview with the police, he felt his skin start to crawl with dread. Had Satan found him at last? The skeleton he'd buried all those years ago it would seem, had escaped the darkest closet of his subconscious. Helpless to prevent it running amok among the catacombs of his troubled mind, he felt a band of tension tighten around his forehead and a formidable weight bearing down on his shoulders. For some odd reason his flesh felt sore and every bone in his body ached with regret. Even the saliva in his mouth tasted like it'd turned acidic, a vile, repugnant substance which burned as it seeped down through his entrails. The weather was perfectly lovely, warm and pleasant, but he found his progress slow and sluggish, hindered to a great degree by his own negative thoughts, as if he was struggling head down against an invisible blizzard.

Desperately he sought solitude, for he knew his nerves were now dangling perilously on a ragged edge. He needed to get this business in his head straightened out fast; this aversion of his youthful past. But it hurt him to think of back then. He couldn't bare the memory of it and had no yearning to be reminded of that terrible night. Not now. Not ever!

Even just to imagine his former friend and associate, Giuseppe Machiavelli caused him to cringe in disgust for he was the last person in the world he would want to consider. Resentfully, he thought of all the anxious years in which he'd been left hanging in the dark. Never quite certain of what'd really happened on that sordid night, often laden with feelings of guilt and self-reproach, expecting Interpol to burst into his home at some unearthly time of the night, breaking down the door unannounced. He shuddered at the thought of it all.

The mental anguish it had caused him during his early twenties and the countless sleepless nights. All of it attributed to this one individual whose name he dared never mention again. Not to his friends. Not even to his wife. Not to a living soul!

But his mind was racing in panic, his countenance had formed into one of utter fear and his skin was perspiring abnormally, as though his whole being had nosedived into a crisis. To distract his mind temporarily, he tried to banish his dark thoughts by concentrating his full attention instead around the stranger who had, most likely, fallen to an untimely death.

Stopping at the water's edge, he gazed out over the lake which was so calm and flat he could only compare it to a huge sheet of black ice, as if it had miraculously frozen over in the night. A vast solid surface, tangible and dependable, which one could almost step foot upon and casually stroll right across to the sleepy village on the opposite side of the bay.

The sun had climbed to its highest point and the view of Cassone was even more conspicuous, the churches and all of the cream coloured houses reflecting the sunlight. In the distant hills above the little village, he could see the blue lights of the police vehicles still flashing intermediately, although the sirens had been muted for some time, he noticed.

He wondered if they'd discovered the poor chap yet. Why would anyone do such a desperate thing? Why was it some people felt this reckless need to end their lives in such a dramatic fashion? At least this guy, whoever he was, had thought to spare the nerves of some unsuspecting bus driver or train driver. Ralph thought it best to evict these gloomy thoughts from his head, dismissing them all as irrelevant. Gradually he began to settle down.

Ambling along the shore, he tried his utmost not to think of anything at all, until he'd slipped into such a deep, meaningless contemplation that he'd hardly noticed the tiny olive-skinned hand tugging on the back of his t-shirt. Turning around slightly curious, he initially thought nobody was there before he peered down and saw a little girl in her wet bathing costume. She was stood still with her hands tucked behind her back, smiling up at him cow-eyed. Her bright blue eyes were as large as coat buttons.

The delicate child, of maybe five or six years, said something to him in her native tongue which he could hardly comprehend. The angelic expression on her tiny face was the epitome of innocence, he thought, and all that was good and decent in this sometimes-ugly world. 'I'm so sorry,' Ralph explained, in his softest tone of voice, 'but I don't understand you.'

Despite his ignorance, the little girl had somehow already sensed his unhappiness. She smiled up at him again, caringly and gave him her best pebble - it was shiny, about the size of a sparrow's egg and reddish-brown in colour. Ralph accepted her kind gift and returned her loving smile. He was reminded of his own dear daughter when of a similar age, a precious memory when she too had collected shells at the seaside for her daddy to keep. His heart grew warm as the little girl skipped away back to her parents, happily humming some nursery rhyme to herself.

5

Meanwhile, across the bay in the green hills above Cassone, several men in dark blue and red uniforms from the local police were busy combing the cordoned off area directly beneath the crag, above which stood the landmark Machiavelli estate. Working directly under the inspector's orders, they were meticulously searching in between every blade of grass and random crack in the rocks within the vicinity with the aid of an Alsatian sniffer dog. When the inspector and sergeant arrived however, the officer in charge of the small search party had so far nothing to report.

The two plain-clothed policemen exchanged looks of disbelief and stared up at the house on top of the cliff with puzzled expressions. The inspector opened a fresh packet of chewing gum and offered his sergeant a piece.

'Well, what do you suppose has happened here then, Bellini?'

Gazing up at the great height of the overhanging rocky ledge, his assistant replied, pessimistically, 'absolutely nothing sir!' He felt quite resentful, having sacrificed his day off. 'I don't believe there is a body, there can't be sir.' He added, appreciating the great effort his colleagues had made already. 'I think this Ashton character has made the whole thing up.'

Inspector Leopardi paused for a moment, allowing himself time to dwell on the matter. During the short car journey here, they'd spoken about the Englishman. He'd seemed sincere enough, the sergeant had remarked. Intelligent and level-headed, his boss had observed. Both men however, had picked up on his odd behaviour after the inspector had unwittingly mentioned the Machiavelli family, also noticing that his wife too had cottoned on to something fishy about his altered manner.

'I'm not altogether certain, Bellini,' the inspector said, convinced that this case was more intricate than it seemed. 'There's more to this than meets the eye.'

'What are we going to do then, boss?' the sergeant asked, rather frustrated and wanting to throw the book at the Englishman for wasting valuable police time, especially his!

'Patience, my friend,' the inspector replied. 'You better ask the men to now check every grove and every surrounding patch of barren land. If necessary we'll do a house-to-house enquiry, starting with those farmhouses over there, continuing all the way down to the village. They can knock on every bloody door if necessary, I want that person found!'

'But surely, sir,' the sergeant objected. 'You don't still think there's a body, do you?'

'I'm not sure what to think!' the inspector retorted. Although he also had his grave doubts about this *Signor* Ralph Ashton, something in his blood was telling him that the Englishman had told the truth. 'Just do as I ask, please.'

Personally, the sergeant couldn't see the point of continuing with this charade but kept his opinions to himself. 'OK, right you are, sir. I'll see to it straight away.'

6

Still a shade restless, Ralph continued to walk alongside the lake, rolling the child's pebble around between his forefinger and thumb. He knew it was a big mistake coming back to Italy, especially to here of all places; to the very same spot where he and his old friend, Giuseppe Machiavelli, had parted company.

But what could he have done to have avoided this now potentially dangerous situation? Practically nothing! If he'd refused outright and insisted they went to the West Country instead, as they usually did, then his wife would have felt sorely devastated, that's not to say suspicious.

He'd already got away with avoiding this country for the past twenty-odd years or so and therefore hadn't wanted to push his luck. She'd plainly set her heart on Italy though and so consequently there wasn't much he could have done about it, except keep reassuring himself that it was merely a coincidence that she'd chosen this country in the first place, and an even bigger twist of fate that she'd veritably settled on Val di Sogno, the Bay of Dreams.

Soon he came upon a deserted part of the shoreline near the end of the bay where it was perfectly still and peaceful.

He sat down on a large boulder and stared vacantly into the crystal-clear water with the warmth of the sun on his back. All he could hear now was the murmur of the bees, gathering pollen from the flowery brushwood behind him and the soothing wash of the surf gently lapping ashore on the sun-kissed sand.

At last he was able to drop his shoulders and relax a little but try as he might he found he couldn't avoid thinking about his long-lost friend, Giuseppe Machiavelli. Two inoffensive nouns that when placed side by side spelled out disaster. It was impossible to erase the name from his turbulent mind and he sighed, regretfully. Nobody, he knew, could change what had already happened. The past was indelible, and he knew that he had to accept this, lest his life should forever remain in limbo. Reluctantly, he finally surrendered his resistance and allowed his subconscious to begin the process of forwarding the substance of his inner conflict.

After graduating from Portsmouth University, at the beginning of summer 1990, Ralph took his year out with the sole purpose of travelling to as many European states as he possibly could, before eventually trying to find a proper job in England within his chosen profession. One such country was Italy, where he'd visited Rome and Naples in the south and Milan, Venice and Florence and the lakes of the north. However, this had been under very different circumstances altogether, staying in cheap, flea infested rooms in run-down apartment blocks. Back then, for most of the time, he'd had to live hand to mouth. Getting temporary employment whenever and wherever he could, waiting on tables, bartending, hand washing cars, minding pedaloes and even selling wafers of ice cream on the beach, all to sustain the snippets of freedom in between. But then his prospects suddenly took a surprising turn for the better. This had happened on the day when he first encountered Giuseppe Machiavelli, whilst temporarily employed as a bar waiter working at one of the restaurants in Val di Sogno.

Giuseppe had got into a brawl with a drunken tourist. The Norwegian was almost twice his size and would have undoubtedly beaten the young Italian to a pulp if Ralph hadn't intervened. After the fight had been properly diffused the Scandinavian was barred for life, Giuseppe was much the celebrated hero and Ralph, rather unjustly, was dismissed on the spot. So, in an instance, once again, he'd found himself as an unemployed pauper. Despite this, however, he was soon to discover that his new-found friend was in fact the sole heir to the fortune of a very rich and prestigious family. Giuseppe, spoiled by good looks and full of confidence, had never physically worked before or indeed felt any academic urge to further his education. As far as he was concerned, he'd had no need to. He was the playboy son of a playboy millionaire and his only purpose in life was to live his life. Henceforth the pair became inseparable, enjoying their precious days of youth and liberty spontaneously seeking thrills and amusement, exploring everything the lakes and mountains had to offer. The young men, roughly of the same age, naturally became the best of friends.

Overhead, swooping low, a noisy reconnaissance helicopter of the Italian Air Force roared by, enroute to Cassone. The din of the chopper swiftly hooked Ralph out of his trance and brought him straight back to the reality of latter day Italy. For a moment, he'd thought perhaps the helicopter was involved in the search operation before it veered off to the right and continued in a southerly direction. He slipped the little girl's stone into his pocket, picked up another from the ground and threw it into the water. As he watched the ripples of his secret past peter out across the lake, he uttered under his breath, 'Damn you, Giuseppe!'

7

After her husband had gone off for his walk, Grace returned to the room and took the opportunity of savouring a long and relaxing shower. Afterwards, she'd applied a minimal amount of makeup, before dressing casually in her favourite pair of denim jeans which she'd complimented with a loose fitting plain white blouse.

Even though she hadn't really been able to concentrate much, she'd then spent the next couple of hours sitting out on the balcony, writing postcards and reading her magazines. She'd again become rather concerned about her husband's state of mind. He'd seemed rather disturbed earlier when questioned by the police, which had upset her a little bit.

They'd already been here for a week, but he'd only just really started to relax properly. In her opinion he had, in recent months, been working far too hard and she'd noticed the tell-tale signs of someone over-doing it. Fearing for his health, she'd despaired over the possibility of him suffering a coronary heart attack or a stroke. She'd already seen her own parents suffer in this awful manner and was determined not to allow her husband to deteriorate in the same way. The hectic lives they were leading at present were a far cry from the ones like old Riley's that she'd always imagined. And because of this she'd been dropping heavy hints recently on the idea of them gradually giving up work altogether.

But this wasn't something she hadn't properly thought about, she'd spent month after month carefully deliberating and weighing up all the pros and cons of a completely new way of life that she hoped would very much benefit them both, particularly her husband's mental state of·mind – if only she was able to calm him down enough to make him see the sense in it. It'd already taken all her cunning and powers of persuasion to coax him into agreeing with this vacation and the last thing she wanted right now was for him to become anxious again.

At four twenty she answered the telephone in the room. 'Hello.'

A young woman spoke, '*Buona sera Signora*, this is reception calling.'

'Hello, yes.'

'*Scusi Signora, per favore*. Could I speak with *Signor* Ashton?'

'No, I'm afraid he's not here. Can I help you? I'm Mrs Ashton.'

'*Per favore*, when will he be available? There's someone waiting in reception to see him, detective sergeant Bellini from Malcesine *polizia*.'

Grace raised her eyebrows, 'Oh I see, please ask the sergeant to wait a moment, I'll come down myself.' She informed her, naturally volunteering as messenger.

The caller then said, '*Si Signora, ciao,*' before she heard the receiver click back into the dialling tone.

A few minutes later Grace Ashton shook hands with the

young plain-clothed policeman. 'Hello sergeant Bellini, have you any news for us?'

'*Buona sera, Signora*. Is your husband not around?'

'He's gone for a walk officer. I think everything had rather upset him. But I'm sure he'll be back quite soon if you'd care to wait. I'll order some coffee if you like.'

The sergeant seemed a bit put out and couldn't be bothered to waste any more of his valuable time. 'No, *grazie,* I must inform you, *Signora,* that we haven't managed to locate this man of yours.'

Grace gasped, rather surprised. 'But that doesn't make any sense, sergeant. No one could survive such a fall. He couldn't have just got up and walked away.'

'*Si*, I agree, *Signora*. But I can assure you that no such person has been found. Our men have made a thorough search of all the land and property beneath the estate as well as making some strenuous enquiries in the surrounding district.'

'And you've come up with nothing?' she said flatly.

'*Si*, nothing,' he confirmed. 'It seems that this whole hullabaloo has been a pointless exercise and a complete waste of police time,' he added, rather begrudgingly.

Grace pouted her gloss covered lips and shrugged her shoulders. 'Then I'm sure I don't know what to think.'

After a brief pause in their conversation, trying to elicit more information, he asked, 'Tell me *Signora*, had your husband been drinking this morning?'

'Only a glass or two of *Gropello* I think,' she replied, resentfully.

'What about medicines, is he currently taking any kind of medication?'

'Just a pill each night for his cholesterol but that wouldn't cause him hallucinations sergeant. You think he's a head case, don't you?' she retorted, taking offence at the policeman's line of questioning. 'My husband's not a liar you know!'

'No, no, of course not *Signora,*' he said, making light of his comments. 'I'm merely pointing out that sometimes…' He paused again, 'Sometimes the haze over the lake can be quite deceptive and occasionally it is possible to see things which are not really there.'

'So in other words you and your boss, inspector… thingy-majig, believe that my husband's a screwball then!' she fired back in retaliation. 'Well God help the pair of you if there *is* someone lying over there dead or injured!' she added finally, before blatantly storming off in a huff.

The detective sergeant then asked the receptionist to provide him with photographic copies of both Mr and Mrs Ashton's European passports.

8

When Ralph got back to the hotel, he found his wife sitting on a tall barstool sipping a large gin and tonic, her second. Guessing that something was obviously amiss, he pulled up a stool beside her, kissed her lightly on the cheek and ordered himself a glass of beer. 'Hello, darling.'

'Hi love,' she replied, a little downcast. Then she remembered, 'How's your headache?'

Ralph quickly dismissed it, having fibbed about it in the first place, as a triviality and conveniently changed the subject by asking if she'd heard any news of the fallen man.

'Oh, God yes that sergeant whatshisname?'

'Bellini.'

'Yes, sergeant Bellini. He'd called here about,' she glanced up at the clock above the bar, 'about an hour ago, bloody cheek of the fella.'

Ralph pulled an expression of puzzlement, imploring her to enlighten him.

'Well, he kind of implied that they thought you were nuts, like you'd invented the story yourself. Then he'd asked me impertinent questions such as, had you been drinking or

41

are you on any kind of medicinal drugs, as though suddenly you're the villain.'

'They obviously haven't found anyone then!' Ralph exclaimed, extremely annoyed at the idea that the police now seem to regard him as some sort of deluded idiot.

Grace, already a little tipsy, sipped some more of her G and T. 'No, and apparently they'd painstakingly searched everywhere. He seemed really annoyed about that, something about us wasting everybody's time.' She paused for thought, 'I think they're disinclined to believe you Ralph.'

'Is that it then? Have the police just given up with the search?'

'He didn't say…but it sounds like it.'

Ralph now plainly understood that he must have been the only person to have witnessed the mysterious man's leap of death. Perhaps, in retrospect and regardless of his own concerns about the police, he may have fared better had he attempted to stir his wife from her slumber when he'd first noticed the guy, even though she was the only person who still had complete faith in him. Or perhaps he could have distracted the barman's attention or indeed any number of the other guests that had all been sunbathing at the time.

Thinking back, no one else around had seemed at all bothered or troubled by the sad event for evidently it had unfolded before his eyes alone. Picturing the scene once more, he recalled everything was pretty much as it normally was. Boats were sailing across the lake, children were busy building their sandcastles on the beach, old timers in their summer hats were dozing on the benches along the promenade and the ice cream vendors, as usual were singing and selling their delicious cones. Scattered all along the shore, paddling and swimming or just soaking up the warmth of the sun, were scores of other holidaymakers – each of them completely unaware of the tragedy unfolding in their midst.

Disappointed with the sergeant's comments, Ralph sank into a lethargic mood, for as well as worrying about his own predicament he remained emphatically concerned about the stranger's plight. 'And what did you have to say about it all?' he asked, discerningly.

Grace beamed at him before she replied, slurring her words a little, 'Well, I let him know that I didn't take too kindly to some stroppy little upstart denouncing my husband.'

Ralph returned her smile, acknowledging her love and loyalty. 'I've half a mind to go and search for the poor fellow myself, Grace, if only to prove my own credibility.' He said, before finishing his beer and regretting that he was no longer young and compulsive. He then turned to his wife again and smiled at her endearingly. 'You believe me don't you darling,' he said, while gently coercing her to her feet.

'Of course I do, Ralph,' she replied. Then, almost losing her balance, she added, 'I love you.'

'I love you too my darling Grace,' he told her, before slowly leading her by the hand back to their room. Behind the closed door they gazed into each other's eyes and gently kissed before melting into each other's arms. Moments later they slipped beneath the cool, fresh sheets in a naked embrace and made love for the first time in months.

9

Wearing matching *his* and *hers* white towelling bath-
robes and flip flops, provided with compliments
by the Maximillian, the Ashtons were relaxing out on the
balcony. There was a slight breeze adding to their comfort as
they lazily enjoyed the onset of dusk over a glass of chilled
white wine.

As far as Ralph was concerned the setting was just heav-
enly, everything about the world in which he lived now
seemed unparalleled and quintessentially perfect. He'd been
reminded of how good his wife's love and intimacy could
make him feel and just how wonderful their relationship
could be sometimes.

He gazed at her intently, full of admiration, her eyes were
closed, and her head was lent back against the chair. She
seemed to be smiling inwardly and her loving expression
summed up exactly how he was feeling himself. He hadn't
felt like this in a very long time, for years in fact, a consum-
mate sense of just being alive. She was right; they had both
been in want of a decent holiday.

She'd been making a lot of fuss recently about the possibility of them both retiring early, and he was beginning to

think that that might not be a bad idea after all. Perhaps now was the right time to give the notion some serious consideration. Dropping out of the rat race maybe wasn't such a bad thing, he thought. Sometimes, one can easily lose sight of the more important things in life. One should work to live, not the other way round.

For a while, at least, he'd managed to override his troubles and see them through a fresh perspective that is until his wife had felt the need to question him. Right from the very moment the two police detectives had left them alone on the sun terrace, something had begun to play on her mind. However, not wanting to spoil the mood, she said to him gently, 'Ralph.'

'Umm.'

'What was the matter with you then?'

'When was that?'

'You know, earlier, when the police were talking to us.'

'I don't know what you mean, Grace,' he returned, stalling for time, knowing full well that she was trying to prise things out of him. He was aware she was probing and he was wary of her uncanny aptitude to read his thoughts.

'Well, you seemed afraid of something or other, terrified almost.'

Hopelessly groping the back of his mind, he searched for a satisfactory answer with which to pacify her concern, 'Er…Did I?'

'Yes, when that inspector whatshisname said something about that place over there.' As she said this, Grace stared over in the direction of the Machiavelli estate. 'You suddenly became alarmed.'

Ralph said nothing and stared absently across the lake at the lights coming on in Cassone.

'I never mentioned it at the time,' she continued, 'because I could plainly see that you were upset and ruffled, but is everything all right, Ralph?'

'Yes of course love, everything's just fine with me. But you know what I'm like, Grace. People in authority put me on edge, always have.' This was no exaggeration on his part and to a certain extent there was a vein of truth in what he'd just said. Ever since his return from Europe, back in his post student days, he'd grown very distrustful of the police in general, avoiding them at all costs, as if they were his enemy.

'Really, Ralph?' she persevered, convinced that he was holding something back. Although he'd put on a brave face, she'd noticed the look in his eyes had become furtive.

'Yes, really Grace, at the airport for example, even just walking quite innocently through the custom's *Nothing to Declare* aisle somehow got me paranoid and I started to feel guilty for some silly reason.' He was conscious of trying desperately to wriggle out of the hole that he'd unwittingly fallen into. He knew the explanation he'd put forward was a lame excuse, but it was the only thing he could think of in the spur of the moment.

Grace had listened sympathetically to her husband's argument, but he wasn't yet entirely vindicated. She still held doubts regarding his odd and unusual behaviour this afternoon but for the sake of preserving the status quo she decided to accept his meagre defence, at least for the time being.

10

Later, over dinner, Ralph began to deliberate whether he should tell his wife all about Giuseppe Machiavelli. After all, she was his only true friend and she deserved to know.

But his former association with this person had long become a sensitive matter, something he'd struggled to even contemplate let alone discuss with his wife. It was an awkward problem which required a certain amount of tact. He knew that his wife was conversant about him having already been to Italy many years ago, but she remained ignorant to the fact that he'd stayed here, in nearby Malcesine.

He hadn't wanted to tell her, preferring instead to let sleeping dogs lie. He hesitated. Would she not be cross with him though, never having mentioned this before? Would the fact that he'd withheld this thing from her for so long now cause a serious rift in their marriage? A happy marriage which he dared not put at risk. Or would she instead see it in another way and appreciate the reality that he was entrusting her with his life?

Again, his mind insisted on taking him back…

Acquainted for some weeks already, Giuseppe had invited his English friend to come and stay with him for the weekend on his father's private yacht which was conveniently anchored out in the bay of Sogno. His father was abroad for a few days which meant that they'd got the luxurious boat all to themselves. Neither of them had mastered the art of sailing, nevertheless this wasn't construed as any form of hindrance for their only intention was simply to remain in the bay; to relax and have as much fun as possible. Their activity agenda comprised only the basics, namely; swimming, eating, and getting drunk and lazing around in the sun. And indeed, if either of them did happen to feel that little bit more energetic than perhaps even a spot of fishing might suffice. They would be just like real brothers, Giuseppe promised.

Ralph had been delighted to have the chance to play the part of a tycoon's son, even if it was only for a couple of days. He hadn't the slightest inkling though of his friend's insidious ulterior motive. With hindsight, maybe he had *been somewhat naïve for a twenty-two-year-old. He recalled how Giuseppe was always making up some excuse or other to dump 'these tarts' and sneak off to even better bars and night clubs where he promised the women were of a much better class and more to his liking by which time, of course, they'd end up too intoxicated to even attempt to flirt with the girls let alone make love. But Ralph hadn't the foggiest notion that his friend was in fact homosexual and had always assumed his kindness and generosity simply as recompense for his help in the restaurant bar on the night when the Norseman had gone berserk.*

After dining on *lavarello*, lake trout, Ralph and Grace Ashton retired to the lounge bar for brandy and coffee.

Grace felt excited at the prospect of finally achieving one of her lifetime's ambitions. Even though Ralph had paid very little attention to her, she had spoken of nothing else during the meal other than the forthcoming trip to Venice. 'Why the sad face, Ralph?' she asked, after noticing him staring vacantly and feeling a little sorry for him. 'You seem a bit depressed.'

'Oh, I'm sorry love, is it that obvious?' he returned, still brooding over his dilemma about whether he should bite the bullet and bring her totally into his confidence. This was certainly an opportune moment for him to finally come clean and probably the best he was going to get. But he lacked the courage; he couldn't bring himself to tell her the truth. He was too afraid of losing her. 'Oh, it's that smarmy sergeant,' he explained, again diverting his thoughts away from the past. 'I just cannot get my head around what he'd said to you.'

'Don't let it upset you darling, the man's just a buffoon.'

'Well I'm not retracting my statement, Grace. I saw what I saw. That poor guy's still up there somewhere, I'm sure of it! He can't have just vanished, like the ground had suddenly opened up and swallowed him whole. It just doesn't make sense, love.' He quickly dropped the subject when they were joined by their usual dinner companions, Mr and Mrs Meadowbank – whom were also thrilled and delighted to be accompanying them on the trip tomorrow. The coach was going to pick them up at eight o'clock in the morning and would bring them back at approximately eight in the evening.

Stuart and Fiona Meadowbank had been out touring around the lake and had already eaten but were both itching to catch up on the latest news. Fiona, having just been fed a morsel of the day's extraordinary event from the young woman on duty at the reception desk, was bursting to find out exactly what had happened earlier on the terrace and felt somewhat peeved with herself for having missed out on all the excitement. 'Hello you two,' she cried. 'What's all this I hear about a flying man with no clothes on then?'

Grace emitted a soft chuckle, 'A flying what?' Who's told you that?'

Fiona Meadowbank, a bubbly, likeable brunette in her early fifties, hurriedly sat down on the comfortable sofa alongside her friends. 'The young girl did, round at reception. She's been trying her best to explain the details of all the commotion today. We sort of got the gist of it, but please do fill us in,' she pleaded, craving for gossip.

'Want a drink, Stuart?'

'Don't mind if I do, Ralph.'

'Brandy?'

'Yes please.'

'And do you want the same, Fiona?'

'Oh yes please, dear. But Ralphy darling, please do put us out of our agony and tell us what the devil has happened here!' she exclaimed, in a playful mode.

Ralph gave the barman the order for his friend's drinks and then proceeded to explain, 'Well, it wasn't nothing much really, this bloke fell off the roof of one of those houses across the bay, that huge mansion up in the hills.'

'Really Grace, I could strangle your husband sometimes! *Nothing much*, he says. From what I've heard the man was absolutely starkers!' She followed this up with a brief dirty laugh, adding as an afterthought, 'Must have been a sight for sore eyes, I'd imagine.'

Grace smiled, amused by her friend's remark. 'Well, yes that's true, Fiona, he didn't have a stitch on, but seriously, Ralph thinks the guy has taken his own life.'

'Committed harakiri, do you mean?'

Ralph elucidated further, 'He was standing right at the very edge of the flat roof with his arms spread out like this.' Once again, he imitated the man's posture. 'It appeared to me like he'd climbed up there with only one purpose in mind... And then when the church bells had stopped ringing, you know the ones that we hear every day at noon, over he went.'

'Oh I say, how intriguing,' Fiona remarked, lapping it up. 'Did you see him as well, Grace?'

'Well no, to be perfectly honest with you Fi, I was away with the fairies, zonked out on the sun bed, when Ralph brought it to my attention.'

Stuart Meadowbank, a staid and respectable type, then asked, 'And what have the police done?' He was handing his excited wife one of the brandies which the barman had fetched over. 'I take it you've informed the police?'

'Of course we have,' Ralph returned, now almost wishing that they hadn't. 'We're not fools you know.' Chatting to his friends had helped to dilute his negative outlook and he began to perk up.

'Not a lot, to be frank,' Grace said, before suddenly back-pedalling with her remark. 'Well no, that's not strictly true. To be fair they did respond rather promptly after the manager's distress call and judging by the amount of flashing blue lights we saw over there along with all the sirens we heard, they'd obviously put a lot of time and effort into trying to locate the man. But believe it or not they haven't found anyone yet.'

'How bizarre,' Fiona commented, consuming her liquor faster than she would normally have. 'Do you know what I think has happened, I reckon some old maid up there has taken him in and kept him to herself, hiding him up like some fugitive.'

Scowling at his wife with daggers of contempt, Stuart Meadowbank then said in a firm tone of voice. 'Assuming the poor fellow is now dead, I shouldn't have thought it too difficult a task to come up with the body by now.'

'I know,' Ralph agreed. 'That's the oddest thing of all, Stuart. So far, they've found absolutely zilch. And to make matters worse, Grace reckons that they now consider me to be nothing more than a blithering imbecile. I shouldn't be surprised if they turn up here before long and arrest *me* now, for wasting their time and resources.'

'So it's watch this space then,' Fiona concluded, gulping down the remainder of her brandy, having thoroughly enjoyed all of the banter.

'Yes, it would seem so,' Ralph agreed, who was now more inclined to clam up about the unfortunate episode, dismissing the whole palaver as a rather regrettable experience.

Following some additional consideration of the matter however, Stuart Meadowbank said, a little conceitedly, that he thought it all could quite easily have been a practical joke, a put-up job.

Ralph silently considered this idea as rather implausible, but Grace wanted Stuart to clarify his remarks. He then further insinuated that this whole travesty was probably nothing more than a clever prank, performed by some capable individuals with a perverse sense of humour. Things like this happen all the time, he said.

Over another round of drinks their discussions were mainly centred on the Meadowbank's exceptional day which they'd spent touring around some of the lake's towns and villages. They'd visited the leather market in Bardolino, the castle in Sirmione and sampled the delights of Garda itself. Both Grace and Ralph agreed it sounded like a lot of fun and vowed to do something similar themselves before their holiday was over. When they finished their drinks Stuart proposed, bearing in mind tomorrow's early start, that it was probably wise to retire for the evening. On this point they were all agreed.

11

Grace fell asleep almost instantly, but Ralph tossed and turned and struggled to relax. He found it impossible to sleep for again his mind was spinning with thoughts of the past. Eventually he got up, slid the patio door ajar and quietly slipped out into the coolness of the night and leaned out over the balcony.

Distorted echoes of merriment coming from the partygoers around the bay were drowned out by the slightly more dominant sound of the surf on the beach below, although only gently sloshing ashore it was nonetheless soothing and calming. Staring out at the reflection of the full moon, beaming down onto the lake's surface like a theatre's spotlight, he imagined himself out there now – floating naked on his back within the circle of brilliant light, adrift on the cold water and gazing up at the mass of orbs in the night sky marking the celestial boundaries of time. Slowly, he felt himself drifting back to another time...

Their last night on the boat had been one of flippancy and fun. They'd danced and sang and sky-larked about like a pair of court jesters, having both got gloriously drunk on some of

Signor *Machiavelli senior's finest champagne. They'd eaten his rainbow trout, smoked his Cuban cigars and giggled about all the great times they'd shared already.*

The gullible young English adventurer however, hadn't become quite as drunk as Giuseppe had contrived to get him. In the small hours, Ralph had woken up in his own cabin, stone-cold sober and fully aware that he was no longer alone. Lying down in the darkness, he could feel somebody's hot and excited breath on the skin of his bare back and that same person's naked, sweating body pressing down hard against his own exposed buttocks. 'What the hell is this!' he shrieked. With the shocking realisation that he was actually about to be raped, he heaved himself up in a frantic rage and was easily able to throw off his assailant.

There was a loud crash to the floor and as he groped for the lamp switch he heard the perpetrator groan in pain. Aghast by the appalling sight of his friend lying naked flat on his back, evidently still clearly excited by the sexual intent he'd had in mind, Ralph was flabbergasted beyond belief. For a moment he refused to trust what his eyes were seeing and would rather have believed himself part of some diabolical nightmare. But his eyes remained transfixed, too afraid to blink, fearing it all devastatingly real. Desperately, he tried to gather up the remnants of his thoughts, which had taken fright and scattered to every vacant nook of his brain. Giuseppe remained motionless in the same awkward position in which he'd landed and just smirked brazenly. Ralph felt outraged, betrayed and indescribably hurt.

Quickly he yanked up his underwear from around his thighs, slipped on his shorts, t-shirt and sandals and, without uttering a single word, made a hasty exit to the outer deck. Giuseppe, only moderately embarrassed, emphatically begged him to stay, blaming it all on the champagne, crossing himself and swearing an oath that it would never happen again. It was just a moment of madness, he assured him.

Ralph refused to have anything more to do with him. He'd never felt so incensed and was on the verge of retaliating, but he couldn't decide whether he ought to black his eyes; to bloody his nose, or just to call him every obscenity under the sun. He wondered how long his friend had been planning all of this. Everything was beginning to make sense now, he thought, his sulks and mood swings and the fact that he'd never introduced him to any other member of his family, nor indeed to any of his friends and associates. He'd often thought it a bit strange as well, why Giuseppe had always seemed to prefer his sole company, which at times had been blatantly obvious and not to say a trifle suffocating. In fact, now he'd had the opportunity to think about it, he recalled that since they'd teamed up, he'd seldom wanted to mix with anyone else.

His friend's sexuality was of course his own affair, Ralph conceded. But how on earth did he think he'd get away with this? The thought of Giuseppe, the best friend he'd ever had, capable of even considering such a notion made him feel sick to his stomach. He knew he had to get off this boat and fast!

Giuseppe was desperate not to lose his best friend and once again beseeched him to stay. 'But you don't understand, I love you Ralph,' he pleaded. 'Please don't go, please...'

Listening to his friend degrade himself in such an undignified manner physically sickened Ralph, even though he loved him too but in a very different way, rather like the brother that he'd always wanted. And not that he'd held any homophobic views either, Ralph believed that he possessed no prejudice whatsoever, having always considered himself a citizen of the world where everyone was his equal and either his brother or his sister.

But he dreaded to think of what might have been if he

hadn't woken up fully in charge of his faculties. His best friend, unbelievably, had planned to violate his body whilst he was unconscious, wrongly assuming that he'd be too inebriated to know anything about it, something which he would never forgive him for.

'I love you,' Giuseppe cried repeatedly, trying his utmost to drag Ralph back out of the rubber dinghy, genuinely distraught at the prospect of losing his best friend forever.

'Look, just get lost will you!' Ralph cried, torrid and struggling to separate himself from his potential rapist. He couldn't tolerate his touch a moment longer. Everything about his friend filled him with a sickening disgust. Even the tone of his voice now sounded tinged with deceit. Giuseppe had destroyed everything, his hope, his plans, his very happiness, all of it gone in an instant. As far as Ralph was concerned normality had been turned on its head, the dream like existence he'd enjoyed of late suddenly swept aside by a flood of lies and twisted truths. No amount of pleading and grovelling was going to prevent him from leaving now. The high esteem in which he'd held his friend was irretrievably lost. 'I hate you Giuseppe!'

Then, quite erratically, as if his dearest friend had suddenly become superfluous to his own emotional needs, Giuseppe, bolt eyed and frenzied, lashed out at Ralph in a vicious, unprovoked, attack, slapping and scratching and pulling at his hair, somewhat effeminately.

Unable to maintain their balance on the dinghy, bobbing on the water, they toppled overboard locked arm in arm in combat. Beneath the cold, dark water Giuseppe was the first to panic, their bodies parting as he desperately tried to resurface, coming up and clouting his head hard on the underside of the yacht. In the next moment he was gone and Ralph saw no further sign of him.

A boat returning to the jetty suddenly boosted its light capacity and loudly sounded its horn, which jerked Ralph firmly back into the present. With much dismay he found himself having to clasp his own arm to stop himself shaking, his heart was pounding irregularly and his whole body was soaked in sweat. To regain his composure, he chose to concentrate solely on his breathing; inhaling and exhaling more steadily – regulating the pattern, gradually lessening the panic.

Loitering among the cobwebs of his misty memory, he felt for a moment as though he'd become entangled in a giant arachnid's lair, trapped between the realms of veracity and fantasy. Did it all really happen quite like that, on the boat? He pondered; doesn't one's recollection become more indeterminate over time? Bedevilled with doubt, he began to challenge his own interpretation of those earlier memories, but the traumatic event was so long ago, he could hardly distinguish anymore between truth and fiction. He shook his head to clear the fog but the dark uncertainty remained with him.

Stirring up these thoughts weren't very helpful at all, he had to admit. His mind was confused enough already but to stop himself doing this he knew he needed distraction, some worthwhile challenge engaging enough to take his mind off what'd happened before. The solution, thankfully, was staring him in the face. He promised himself, that just for the time being, he would endeavour to concentrate all his energy on unlocking the paradoxical mystery of the missing man, thereby hopefully allowing himself to focus properly on the present and ultimately to forget the past.

Across the bay Ralph could see the lights of Cassone, above which were the hills in pitch darkness. He imagined the man lying dead there somewhere; his naked body limp and broken, sprawled out on the rocks at the foot of the crag. Had anyone cared about this poor, tortured soul before he'd taken that fatal decision to end his miserable life? he wondered. Did anyone care now?

Ralph inhaled a long, deep breath and sighed in despair, slowly coming to understand that the enigma shrouding the whereabouts of the lost man had started to bother him just as much as the bad memories of his past, which he was so desperately trying to forget.

But something inside him, the oddest feeling, a niggling compulsion, call it what you like, was insisting that he must find this man. He knew it was the right thing to do. Except for his faithful wife, he didn't think anyone had really believed his story and he felt he owed it to himself to prove them all wrong. Accordingly, he now saw it as his own responsibility to seek him out; the anonymous person that nobody else it seemed was prepared to help.

The trip to Venice was set for tomorrow but unfortunately it was also the only realistic day left open to him on which to try and discover, for his own peace of mind, what'd really happened to this mysterious person. He had another dilemma to consider. Should he accompany his wife and friends tomorrow or should he pretend to be unwell? Apart from the little headache fib he'd told her earlier Ralph had never lied to his wife. He hated lies and he despised liars even more so. Nevertheless, needs must, he thought. So somehow, he now had to make an allowance within in his own scruples for the fresh yarn whirling around in his head. To console himself he had to regard the deception merely as an exception to the rule.

Early the following morning his wife would be leaving for

the city and she'd be gone all day. Plenty enough time then, he thought, in which to capture the reassurance he sought. He could feel a dull ache in his chest, as if he'd started to grieve for the missing man. Empathy for the stranger who in all honesty meant absolutely nothing to him and a sense of helplessness that he couldn't quite altogether comprehend. Nevertheless, he felt it was also something which he couldn't discount lightly either, lest it should haunt him for the rest of his life.

By no means did he consider this thing, whatever it was, more important than being with his wife tomorrow but the urge to address it, he felt somewhat intensely, had become impossible to ignore any longer. He stared out at the shimmering waters for a moment or two and felt relieved that he'd made up his mind about one thing at least. He had no intention of going to Venice with his wife and friends tomorrow.

By contrast, come the morning, he would again feign some kind of ailment and beg to be excused. He didn't relish the idea of having to convince Grace though that she should still travel along with the Meadowbanks, irrespective of his sudden illness. But he would remain defiant and insist that he was more than capable of looking after himself. He'd also remind her that he'd already visited the city many years ago, but she hadn't, and he didn't want to feel any worse than he did already.

He knew Grace very much admired Mr and Mrs Meadowbank and Ralph knew he was fortunate that they'd all become congenial friends. They'd spent several pleasant evenings in one and other's company, either at the hotel or at one of the numerous restaurant bars around the bay and discovered that they had much in common. Stuart

Meadowbank was a telecommunications engineer. Fiona Meadowbank, like Grace, was involved in landscape gardening and each of them shared the same tastes in wine, food and music. Coincidently, the Meadowbank couple had never been to Venice either.

12

The following morning at around 6am, Ralph swung his plan into action and promptly began to fidget and sigh, making certain to disturb his wife from her sleep. Knees up to his stomach and clamped in the jaws of his clenched hands, he groaned and grumbled his way through the fantasy illness, complaining of belly ache and feeling sick, possibly a stomach bug. Or more than likely it was the effects of sunstroke, too much exposure yesterday, he proposed.

Initially, Grace had become rather disconcerted about her husband's symptoms and was intent on calling the doctor but as he intentionally began to lessen the affects of his mystery illness she gradually began to calm down. Needless to say, she was far from happy. Venice was off; she insisted and instead had nobly decided to nurse him throughout the day. Proceeding to dab his forehead caringly with a cold, damp face flannel, she promised to get him some medicine for his tummy cramps as soon as the pharmacy opened.

Ralph's ploy was seriously beginning to backfire. Oh hell! He thought, likening his wife to an unwanted modern-day version of Florence Nightingale. 'No Grace, *you* must still go,' he persisted. 'It'll be a dreadful waste of money if we both miss out. And what about Fiona and Stuart, they'd be terribly disappointed, love?'

'Yes, but look at you!' Grace said. 'How can I leave you like this?' she added, but now with her decision to stay with him hanging by a thread. She felt bitterly disappointed that he wasn't able to accompany her on the outing but was more upset about his present condition. All said and done this is why she'd brought him to Italy in the first place; in the hope of improving his health. But maybe he wants to be on his own, she thought, reconsidering the situation. Perhaps I should leave him here; a day in bed would probably do his nerves the world of good.

It had been a very near thing for Ralph had had to tone down his aches and pains almost to the point of a miraculous recovery before his wife finally, but reluctantly, agreed to his wishes. At last, Ralph was able to relax, albeit somewhat clandestinely, as he laid back and watched his wife ready herself for the big day ahead.

It was at times like this when he counted himself a very fortunate fellow indeed, his wife was still a very desirable woman. He studied her admiringly through one half-opened eye, carefully applying her makeup with such delicate precision, sat in her sexy lingerie in front of the dressing table. She'd certainly looked after herself over the years, constantly dieting; regular trips to the gym and of course, sampling every conceivable moisturising product that ever came onto the market. He continued to stare at her privately; content and grateful that she'd consented to be his beautiful bride. Suddenly, he wondered where all of those years had gone and he knew his life meant nothing without her.

13

In the taxi, Ralph felt intense guilt and was wondering whether he'd made the right decision to remain behind. Less than thirty minutes ago, he'd croaked a half-sleepy cheerio to his wife, before hurriedly dressing and sneaking round to the rear of the hotel to watch the coach depart. She'd got a window seat next to Fiona and Stuart and he knew just how happy and excited she must have been feeling.

However, contrary to his wife's elation, Ralph had felt ashamed, considering his deceit almost tantamount to treachery. He knew how much she'd been looking forward to seeing Venice and he felt dreadful, like he had let her down terribly. Skulking around behind the clematis and honeysuckle bushes, like a peeping Tom, had worsened his feelings of guilt but he'd had to ensure that the trip was going ahead and that she was definitely on the bus.

He could feel butterflies in the pit of his stomach and the rest of his insides churning with an unacceptable sense of loss, and just for a brief moment, fearing that he would never see her again, he'd even considered chasing after the vehicle as it slowly began to pull away. Somehow, in the cold light of day, the missing man's whereabouts didn't seem to be that important anymore. Nevertheless, despite his regrets, he'd retreated timidly farther beyond the citrus trees and waved her off surreptitiously until the coach had driven out of sight.

Coming into Cassone, Ralph instructed the driver to stop and let him out, pulling over at the first decent restaurant he happened to set his hungry eyes upon. As a precaution, he'd thought it best to skip his breakfast at the Maximillian. This was just in case Roberto, the senior waiter, happened to unintentionally mention to his wife later that he'd been alone at the dining table. Naturally, if he'd been feeling well enough to scoff down his usual full English breakfast, then it stands to reason that he wouldn't have had any excuse not to have joined them all on the daytrip.

After paying the cabby his fare he sat down at one of the empty tables in the shade under the extended awning and waited patiently to be served. His belly groaned with hunger pains and his mouth was dry but he felt much more at ease, here alone beside the lake out of the way of prying eyes. As he was the only customer, he was attended to more or less straight away by a cheerful young waitress who gladly took his order for some ham and eggs. In addition, he asked for some fresh bread, some coffee and cake and a bottle of chilled mineral water for his walk later.

The morning was perfectly lovely and wonderfully peaceful. He looked up and saw only a smidgen of white cloud, drifting gently across the pale blue September sky as the sun hung low over the misty waters in the bay. There was a whispery breeze in the warming air, the lake dead slow and silent.

He gazed out at the big grey mountain predominant in the distance that seemed to him to exude a mysterious calmness of its own, spilling down the mountainside like invisible lava, penetrating every winding lane, alleyway and *piazza*, sedating the inhabitants under its magical spell. The deserted hamlet struggled to awaken and although his watch told him that it had only just turned eight thirty Ralph wondered, with an emerging sense of envy, if this was pretty much how things normally were.

When he'd finished his meal, he summoned back the waitress and asked for his bill. He complimented the girl on her delicious food and tipped her appropriately, before finally making his way back across the empty square to the far side of the deserted main road. Here he was confronted by the daunting sight of at least a half dozen different routes to consider, spaced out more or less evenly along the narrow street. Fortunately, they all tended to lead in an upward direction, so opting for the nearest pathway, he put on his sun hat and sunglasses and thus began his quest to uncover the truth about the mysterious man, who had apparently vanished so completely and so mysteriously.

14

Striding up through the old village, Ralph couldn't help noticing the popularity of lime trees and pomegranate trees. They were growing everywhere among copious amounts of jasmine and bougainvillea. With a keen interest in horticulture, he was full of admiration. The gardens were spectacular and immaculately kept and the streets were just as clean and tidy. People took pride here.

In *via Chiese*, he passed by the splendid *Domas del et Parta Coeli* Church with its prominent bell tower, domed roof and yellow painted façade. An elderly man with leathery looking skin was sitting on a bench near the entrance gates resting the weight of his weary arms on his cane walking stick. '*Buongiorno*,' he said, before grinning contentedly, exposing his toothless gums.

'*Buongiorno*,' Ralph returned, respectfully. Apart from the jovial young girl who'd served him his breakfast, the old man was the only other person he'd seen in this sleepy village. Not even a bicycle or a car had passed him by. Mindful of this, everything about the place now seemed eerily unreal and forsaken as though he'd just strode into a film studio's make-believe town, every door locked and window shuttered. The place felt as dead as a dodo's mausoleum.

From up here though there was a wonderful view of the lake below upon which, he noticed with much relief, there was some activity at least. Silhouetted against the glare of the sun he could see a few energetic figures windsurfing and jet skiing in their wetsuits and there were others out sailing their boats. Gazing down at the waters, shimmering with flecks of gold and silver, he knew that everything was as it should be. But up here in the hills, he got the feeling that things were far from normal.

A short distance away, in the *piazza Giarola*, he came upon another church, or to be more precise, a small Christian chapel. Ralph's initial impression of this place of worship was one of sadness. It seemed to be in a very poor condition, its exterior plasterwork had been blistered and cracked by the sun and in patches had completely fallen away from the brickwork. The bell tower above seemed broken beyond repair. He couldn't see a notice board or a plaque anywhere to describe its name. Ralph was rather surprised to discover that the little church was in actual fact open for prayer. The main door at the front end had been left wide open, welcoming all that wished to spend some time in this sanctuary of the Lord's. Just to satisfy a passing whim, he stole a glimpse through the porch way and immediately saw a number of lighted candles flickering with life up before the altar. His nose had also detected a strong smell of incense burning; floating on the musky air coming from inside but there didn't seem to be anyone in attendance. He listened for a moment to the divine silence as was unexpectedly overcome with a feeling that he didn't belong here.

Having long excommunicated himself from the Church entirely, for reasons of his own, he stood hesitant on the threshold and mused for a moment. Apart from the occasion of his daughter's wedding, this would be the first time he'd entered any kind of religious establishment since his children's Christenings at the family's parish church in Rochester over two decades ago and he suddenly felt uncomfortable with the idea. He knew his impeccable reputation wasn't so squeaky clean as his family and friends had been led to believe. Ralph the sinner gradually backed away, preferring instead to remain in the Godless world that he was more used to.

Back in the square, he took a sip of water and glanced up at the yellow manor house set among the olive groves. It was farther away than he'd first thought, now appearing much less obtrusive sat high above the ridge. He looked at his watch and then back up at the villa and felt strangely drawn by it, as if he were returning home from a long, arduous journey across hostile and foreign lands, an odd, inexplicable sensation which had taken him several minutes to shake off. But never mind, he told himself, after the unsettling feeling had finally extinguished itself, he had enough water and as long as he paced himself properly he should be able to reach the foot of the crag in good time.

Following several hard and steep climbs up and around the tortuous lane he finally arrived at the beginning of the olive groves. The road he'd been walking, that was hardly wide enough for a single vehicle, he now understood, continued on farther all the way up to the Machiavelli estate. However, now having no wish to go there he left the road and trespassed into the grove. Panting with exhaustion he decided to take a five minute break, straddling a dry stone wall, one of many that divided the terraced groves. He was wondering about what Grace might be doing. His watch said it was 10.42, she'd be in Venice by now, he thought. He was missing her already and once again had grave doubts about his decision to come here. He began to mull things over for a while, mostly blaming himself.

He should have gone along with her instead, he told himself. What did he expect to discover here anyway? If the police couldn't find anything conclusive then why did he believe he could do any better? But the negative thoughts he was experiencing right now were probably just more diversionary tactics, he guessed, a kind of self-defence mechanism in his brain trying to shield him from further distress. For the time being, he knew he had to ignore them and concentrate on what he was doing. There was no sense in giving up now, he concluded. What was the alternative? If he should return to the hotel, what was he meant to do now for the rest of the day, except sit in the room and fret about his wife? Anyhow, he was meant to be ill, he reminded himself. There was nothing else for it other than to continue with his expedition up into the foothills.

Still climbing at a fairly steep gradient, he zigzagged his way through the olive trees looking one way then the other until the ground finally began to level out and where he was also eventually forced to stop.

Mentally, he'd struggled hard to resist this urge to come and search for the missing man, believing that he'd probably be unsuccessful in his mission. His head kept telling him one thing and his heart another. Nevertheless, he was now standing rooted to the ground feeling utterly horrified and completely appalled. For there it was, the body of the naked man, lying exactly where he'd expected it to be all along, at the bottom of the precipice, directly beneath the great, imposing villa towering above.

He'd never seen a dead body before and had never wanted to. Not even when his own parents had passed away had he gone to see them at the chapel of rest. The thought of peering down at either his mother or father in a coffin, looking something like a Madame Tussauds wax-dummy, had filled him with dread. However, none of this though was making any sense. This spot in particular must have been crawling with inspector Leopardi's uniformed officers yesterday. The police cannot be that stupid, he thought. What the blazes was going on? he fretted, now almost annoyed with himself for having found the body.

He proceeded to take a few steps nearer but then suddenly halted again. That's odd, he thought, there didn't seemed to be a scratch on it. He would have thought the body would have been cut to shreds by the sharp, jagged, rocks having plummeted from such a great height. But the body was unscathed and appeared more like one of Michelangelo's nude models rather than someone who'd just fallen off a sixty-foot cliff. No cuts or abrasions; bruise or blemish. This didn't feel right at all. Something was terribly amiss. Erring on the side of caution, he crept up a little closer. The man was laying face-down on the rocky slab, his face still hidden from view.

Feeling dizzy with stress and apprehension, Ralph leant down and lightly touched the apparently dead man's back, the flawless skin stone-cold and deathly pale. But then suddenly his heart leapt up into his throat and shook like a rattlesnake's tail. 'My God!' he yelled, as the 'corpse' jumped up in front of him and bolted away down the hill. 'He's still alive!'

Stunned beyond belief, Ralph sank to his knees and allowed himself a good few minutes in which to catch his breath. Puffing and panting as though he'd just run a marathon, his heart raced with anxiety, pumping blood and excessive amounts of adrenalin around his trembling body. Reeling in shock, he tried to make some sense out of what his eyes had just witnessed. He gazed up at the top of the escarpment and wondered how on earth the man survived. Without doubt the drop from such a height would have killed anyone outright. So why was it then that this man was still breathing? He quizzed himself. Everything seemed incongruous but at the same time all too neat and tidy and Ralph was busting a gut to find out why.

Jumping back to his feet, he drew in a few deep breathes before sprinting off in pursuit, now unexpectedly excited by the chase and intrigued by the extraordinary young man who'd seemingly cheated the grim reaper himself. However, as his brain struggled to analyse what'd happened, he concluded one thing at least. Finding this guy had been far too easy. His effort, he understood, had been no more than superficial but most astonishing of all of course, was the fact that the mystery man has turned out to be alive and well. He had appeared as fit and sprightly as an Olympic athlete.

15

This wasn't the only occasion that something wholly bizarre had taken place since his arrival back in this country. Tracing events back to the middle of last week, when sightseeing in Verona with his wife, Ralph recalled strange incidents concerning the rather debonair young man who'd tailed them around the city like some kind of private detective, only this guy had made his own presence blatantly obvious. The first time he'd noticed this displeasing character was when they were visiting the Colosseum. It was extremely hot that day, he recalled. The streets, usually hectic with droves of tourists, had almost slowed to a standstill; most of the crowds having sought refuge from the scorching sun in the shade of trees or in the coolness of the churches, or under café awnings, or were just stood quietly in the shadows cast by the old buildings.

Inside the great arena, whilst sitting next to his wife on the relatively empty stone terraces, he'd suddenly felt a burning sensation on the nape of his neck, accompanied by a peculiar sense that somebody was ogling him. His suspicion was confirmed when he turned round sharply to investigate and saw the young man staring down at him rather deliberately.

Ralph had peered up at the fellow equally curious for there was something vaguely familiar about his face but was soon forced to avert his eyes because of the sun's intensive glare. Moments later, when his vision had settled back to normal, he stole a further glance up behind him only to learn that the man had gone. Prior to this they'd been admiring the enormity of the monumental building, soaking up its turbulent history over the past couple of millenniums. But now he was feeling a bit put out and struggled for the reason as to why the stranger should have glared at him in such a direct negative manner. There was something evil in that look, he thought, venomous and derogatory, which gave him cause to shiver for a moment like somebody stepping on his grave.

Later that afternoon, contrary to expectation, he came across the same young man again. This time it was in the short passageway which led into Romeo and Juliet's courtyard. Earlier in the Colosseum, because of the blinding sun, he hadn't been able to get a proper look at the guy but was now afforded the opportunity of observing him in full view.

Ralph guessed that he was probably somewhere in his early twenties but he couldn't be absolutely certain for his facial features were now to some extent obscured by the large pair of snazzy shades he was wearing. He was dressed in a royal blue suit tailored from an expensive linen material, a plain white shirt and a pair of highly polished black shoes with pointed toes. Although smart and presentable, his look was still rather unusual as his clothes were not of the styles of the present-day. However, like before, he was persistently staring at Ralph with the same look of disrespect. The young man's attitude was nothing more than a bloody nuisance, thought Ralph, but all the same he felt himself becoming more annoyed with the fellow.

Beneath the famous balcony there is stood a bronze statue. Supposedly, if one was to gently touch the breast of this scantily clad sculptured woman, it will bring the participant good fortune in the concept of love and romance.

Whilst his wife was in the queue, waiting her turn to stroke the lucky lady, Ralph seized upon the chance to address the man face to face. However, to his extreme annoyance, he immediately found his access obstructed by a sudden stampede of enthusiastic Asian tourists, each loaded with an array of photographic paraphernalia and unfortunately by the time he'd fought his way through the crowd, the arrogant young man was again nowhere to be seen.

Remarkably though, the man Ralph had seen had had the audacity to present himself once more that day, along one of the shopping boulevards off the main thoroughfare. Whilst Grace was busy haggling over the price of a designer hat she'd taken a serious liking to, Ralph had noticed him over on the opposite side of the lane.

The man was leaning casually with his arms folded up against a marble statue of some renowned artist of the Renaissance era. Consistent with his earlier condescending behaviour he was eyeing Ralph quite blatantly, almost as if attempting to goad him into some form of confrontation. Ralph knew that beneath those dark lenses the man's eyes were again filled with indignation. Why? He fretted. What possible interest had this anonymous nobody got in him?

Ralph had shrugged off the former episodes as meaningless nonsense but now felt much offended and became even more enraged when the guy began to smirk at him pretentiously. Ralph wanted to wipe that smug smile right off of his face, he thought, already psyching himself up for the possibility of a full on fight. He'd had enough of this nonsense and was determined to resolve the issue with this irksome idiot once and for all. He was aching to know what the blazes this was all about and had already begun to deliberate on how he should tackle the fellow.

However, just when he was about to approach the man, Grace unexpectedly called him into the shop acting as though there was some kind of an emergency. Disappointedly, he swept his anger to one side and naturally rushed to her assistance only to discover that she'd merely wanted to borrow his credit card, having just completed her bargain purchase – an elegant sun hat which she'd success-fully secured at a twenty-five per cent discount. By the time they were finished at the till the man, most confoundedly, had once again disappeared out of sight. Ralph had found the whole episode rather unsettling but as his wife was in such high spirits and rather than ruin her day, he decided that his brushes with this enigmatic young man weren't worth mentioning.

It'd now become apparent to Ralph that the encounters he'd experienced in Verona were merely the beginning of all these weird occurrences.

16

At a steady jogging pace, Ralph had tracked the naked man all the way back down through the olive trees, descending the narrow, twisting lane from one hairpin bend to the next coming into Cassone proper, where he'd noticed him finally run into the nameless chapel in the *piazza Giarola*. As before, everywhere was as eerie as a field in no man's land. Not a murmur could he hear, all sound deadened. Not the cry of a bird, the laughter of a child, not even a breath of wind, like all of a sudden he'd been struck deaf, or else the world had stopped spinning. He crossed the empty, silent square and very gingerly entered the little chapel with no name.

This time, contrary to his own guilt-stricken beliefs, Ralph felt no qualms about breaching the threshold of the consecrated building and duly stepped inside. He was pleasantly surprised however, that he actually felt quite calm and collective and was amazed by the contrasting condition of its interior. It really was quite stunningly beautiful. As well as the scores of candles flickering alight before the sacred altar, which he'd noticed earlier, there were also several more burning in niches and alcoves, where they'd been placed respectfully at the feet of saintly effigies and rustic holy icons. Suspended above the altar was a large wooden cross with a silver crucifixion of Christ. Hung round the walls were numerous exquisite paintings depicting selected biblical scenes and overhead was an awe inspiring ceiling adorned with colourful frescoes telling the story of the death of Jesus on Calvary hill at Golgotha.

The naked man was knelt down before the cross with his hands pressed flat together as in prayer. With exception of the praying man, who seemed much distressed and was weepy noisily, the church was empty. Ralph gradually approached the young man step by step until he'd got within a metre of him. For some unknown reason he then felt lost for what to do or say next, being painfully aware of where he was. But now he'd got this close he had no intentions of letting him out of his sight again. However, in need of a few moments in which to gather his own thoughts and having no wish to intrude on the invoker's prayers, he sat down quietly just behind him on the front row pew, prepared to bide his time until the young man had calmed down.

He was kneeling before the candle-lit altar, seemingly praying for some kind of forgiveness and salvation. What was the terrible sin that he surely must have committed, Ralph pondered, seeing him in such a wretched state? But then suddenly, the young man ceased his snivelling and began to speak, 'Why have you returned, why now?' he asked, 'after all this time?' He'd said this without even bothering to turn around. His head remained respectfully bowed and his hands were still clasped tightly together.

Caught off guard, Ralph struggled for an answer.

'You should not have come back here, you're a fool!' the man exclaimed.

Ralph went straight on the offensive, 'Who on earth are you?'

'Well, you ought to know!'

Somewhat flummoxed, Ralph continued. 'But what…'

'No buts about it,' the impudent young man interrupted. 'You should know very well who I am!'

Annoyed by the juvenile's impertinence and fed up with talking to the back of his head, Ralph promptly stood up to confront him. 'Look here sonny, what's going on? What are you playing at?'

'Who's playing?' the man replied, almost as if he were teasing Ralph. 'This isn't a game, Mr Ashton,' he added acrimoniously.

'You *know* my name?'

'You should not have come back here,' the man repeated, earnestly. 'Now we must both die!'

Ralph couldn't believe what he was hearing and had had just about enough of this insubordinate's malarkey. He grabbed hold of the fellow's shoulder and spun him round by force. What he saw next caused him to recoil in abhorrence and render him practically speechless. He was now gaping at a face identical to his own. He could just as easily have been staring at his own reflection in a mirror glass except it was himself, he recalled, as a twenty-something-year-old. He couldn't work out what was happening, his mind was nothing but a conundrum of confusion.

'Now do you understand?' the young Ralph asked. 'It's me, I am you!' The man's mood suddenly reverted to its former sorrowful state and again he began to weep profusely, shedding tears of blood from eyes poisoned by grief. 'Oh why did you have to come back, Ralph?'

The naked young man then sprang up and burst out of

the chapel in a hopeless panic as if he was trying to escape the Devil himself. Ralph quickly followed him outside and watched him disappear down a narrow alleyway between two derelict buildings. It was noon already and the bells of the larger church lower down the hill were ringing out aloud. When the last of them had finally fallen silent, Ralph could hear nothing else except for the rapid pulsating of his own heartbeat drumming in his inner ears. Reluctant to throw in the towel, he allowed himself a few more minutes to shake off his dizziness before rejoining the hunt. Be it harmless or macabre, something deep in his inner most self was insisting that he kept tabs on this ghost from his past.

The alleyway led him directly into another *piazza* through an ornate pillared marble arch; into a square even more deathly quiet than the last. Ralph was now confronted by the sombre sight of a small cemetery; chock-a-block with marble slabs and stone crosses and encapsulated on all sides by the villager's walled in gardens and courtyards.

Searching among the crowded graves he in time caught up with the phantom of his youthful self. He was kneeling down beside a large, ostentatious mausoleum, mourning the occupants, sobbing dramatically. Ralph, rather shakily, inched towards him in a high state of anxiety before the young man swiftly turned round and beckoned him alongside the grave. Frowning with disappointment, the young Ralph's bloodshot eyes now dripped unrestrained tears of sadness. Pointing at the words graven on the tomb, he wailed, 'Come and see what you did, Ralph. Look, here is your friend, and here is your destiny!'

Then something else very odd indeed began to occur. The apparition of his former self gradually began to fall asunder and dematerialise right before his very eyes. Ralph turned ashen in an instant, as if every last drop of blood had drained from his body. He went rigid with fear, 'What's going on?' he whimpered. Struggling with his equilibrium, he stood swaying to and fro with his face sunk into the palms of his trembling hands, his body numbed with shock from head to toe. Staggering about the graves, giddy with waves of stress and befuddlement, he whined, 'How can this be happening to me?' His head was spinning like a carousel.

Perplexed and fearful he racked his brains for the common denominator between the strange events of late, namely: the psychopathic stalker in Verona, the mysterious suicide and now this spectre of his youth. He couldn't make sense out of any of it but was willing to wager that these things were all somehow linked to the dead man lying beneath the tombstone. Giuseppe Machiavelli's name was etched in black letters into the grey marble stone, next to his father's name and some of his ancestors.

17

Inspector Allesandro Leopardi was standing concealed in the shaded part of the cemetery quadrangle. He'd been secretly observing, with his most undivided attention, the curious behaviour of the man who was fast becoming the object of his intrigue, *Signor* Ralph Ashton.

The inspector, for the latter part of the morning, had been snooping around the Machiavelli estate trying to find some clue, if any, that might connect the house to the Englishman.

However, not long after he'd driven away from the vacant property, he was surprised to notice the same guy, running down the mountain road seemingly chasing shadows like a mad man possessed.

When he'd interviewed *Signor* Ashton yesterday, he'd noticed with interest, how distant he'd suddenly become after he'd inadvertently mentioned the Machiavelli family and yet by the same token how sincere he'd remained about the suicide. Regarding the latter he'd been more than half convinced that the Englishman was telling the truth.

Now he wasn't altogether sure, having listened to the man uttering nonsense to himself and witnessed him chasing something which didn't exist. He'd watched him creeping into the chapel, as if it was packed with explosives and then a short while later saw him rushing out of it again like a drunkard slung out of a bar. Dashing here, darting there. Had the fellow gone mad? And now, finally, he has tailed him to the grave of the young Giuseppe Machiavelli. The son of a tycoon millionaire, who'd sadly drowned in the lake almost a quarter of a century ago when the inspector incidentally, had been on duty that same day as a young officer of the local police force. Because of the suspicious circumstances surrounding the young man's death, the matter, long designated a cold case, has never been entirely closed but has remained inactive. The autopsy findings had revealed that the young man had suffered a blow to his head but had actually died as a result of drowning. The policeman speculated, but what has this crazy man got to do with this long forgotten case?

The inspector had been delving into the past and something was now troubling him deeply. Was the death of this eligible young bachelor all those years ago now somehow connected to a certain *Signor* Ralph Ashton and his mysterious suicide? Something was blinding his intuition; something sinister, he suspected, which he couldn't quite put his finger on. For the time being, through a sheer lack of evidence, he was content to remain beyond the shadows. But from now on he would be keeping a very close eye on this eccentric Englishman.

18

Ralph, full of resentment peered down at Giuseppe's tomb and said softly, 'But you weren't really my friend, were you?' Discovering the grave of his former acquaintance evoked unsolicited thoughts, causing his mind to be wrenched right back to that dark, seedy night almost a quarter of a century ago.

Ralph resurfaced gasping for air. Treading water in the darkness he couldn't see or hear Giuseppe anywhere and there was no sign of the rubber dinghy either. Although seething and upset, he still felt obliged to help his friend but he was nowhere to be seen. Seriously concerned, he began to swim around the boat looking for him. He called out into the black night but Giuseppe was gone. Again he swam around, and again.

Not long after this, Ralph was sitting slumped on the shore close by, soaking wet, shivering with cold and nursing a cramp in his calf. There he stayed with unabated concern, glued to the spot for the remainder of the night, scrutinising every slightest movement upon the lake's surface awash in the moonlight. 'You bastard, Giuseppe!' he cried out, feeling cold, wet and miserable. 'Where are you?'

But Ralph saw no further sign of his friend. 'He must have drowned,' he mumbled to himself. 'He could have swum ashore,' he hoped, clutching at straws. Sitting on his haunches, he embraced himself for warmth. But why should he have gone ashore? He reconsidered the matter. Giuseppe hadn't any clothes on for a start. And he would never have left his father's yacht, not without first making it locked and secure. No, Giuseppe must be dead, Ralph was sure of it. What should he do now though? If he told the police the absolute truth they'd never believe him. The Machiavelli family were the big shots around here and they'd all be baying for his blood. He reminded himself that he was only twenty-two years old and he wasn't going to spend the rest of his life in prison for something he hadn't done. At daybreak he silently slipped away and scuttled back to his austere lodgings, like a rat forsaking a sinking ship, taking great care not to be seen.

The cockroach-infested bedsit that he'd been renting in Malcesine was spartan to say the least. Sometimes he'd thought it more in keeping with a monk's cell. It had a door and a window, four walls and a hard, uncomfortable single bed and not much else. But he knew that beggars couldn't be choosers, the hovel had been cheap to rent.

Ralph had resented the fact that Giuseppe had purposely distanced him from his rich family and friends, almost as though he felt mortified sometimes by his English friend's commonness. But now in the light of what had happened Ralph was thanking his lucky stars for his own poverty. He had never invited Giuseppe back to his own abode either for he'd felt ashamed of the place, which was just as well now in case the police came banging on the landlord's door. As far as he could recall, because of his friend's snobbery, there was no third party *to connect him with Giuseppe Machiavelli, or indeed to any of his associates.*

Giovanni, the skinflint owner of the boarding house, who always wore a grimy, sweat stained string vest and permanently had a lighted cigarette wedged between his lips, wouldn't be around for a few more days yet, demanding his fortnight's rent due, paid in advance. The old miser always insisted on payment in cash, out to diddle the taxman no doubt. He certainly wasn't going to miss his ugly mug and tight-fisted ways. With note-pad and pen to hand, he began to scribble down a few words in Italian explaining that he no longer required the room. However, on second thoughts, he decided that it was probably best if he just left without a word. He tore up the piece of paper and put the fragments into his pocket to dispose of later. There was no need to broadcast his intentions, Giovanni would know.

Without bothering to sleep, he stuffed his few meagre possessions into his rucksack and quietly vacated the run-down building. With the adoration of his friend now in tatters, that he felt certain must have drowned, he scrambled up the steep steps of the cobbled alleyway which led him up on to the main highway. Finally, with his head hung low, his brow mottled in beads of perspiration and his heart racing with fear and yet heavy with sadness, he began to hitchhike his way back across Europe on his long journey home.

In the aftermath of his nerve-racking ordeal, Ralph was sitting stunned in a daze, slumped up against the railings of the Machiavelli family vault. He gazed around vacantly at all of the stone lozenges packed tightly together in long, neat rows, like dusty old volumes in a library, among them no doubt some sad tales of untold tragedy and woe. Each marble tablet marking the earthly remains of a human life already spent, memories bound and forgotten like books out of print.

Struggling to differentiate reality from fantasy, he wasn't even certain anymore about his own state of existence. For the past few hours, he hadn't budged an inch and had done nothing else except remember over and over again what he'd seen. Staring blankly through the cobwebs clinging to the graves, Ralph had tried to work out what on earth was going on. Earlier, he had attempted to leave once or twice but found that he couldn't, forced back each time by an even stronger urge to stay – his ambivalence steering him towards the idea that he should remain beside the burial chamber in the desperate hope that the man would reappear. To see him come back in the flesh from God knows where and confess that everything was just fine and that this awful nightmare was merely nothing more than an elaborate hoax. His weary eyes searched for anything that could be interpreted as a good omen, like a lizard for instance, a dragon-fly, or better still, some rare, beautiful butterfly. He was desperate to see something real and familiar, taking the view that it might just elevate his miserable frame of mind. Alone and afraid, his mood had sunk to an all time low and like a broken man, he sat demoralised, watching the spiders spinning their intricate webs upon which to live out their uncomplex lives. Soon after, exhausted and bewildered, he fell into a fearful slumber.

19

By the time Ralph was finally able to leave the Piazza of the Dead, it was dusk. The autumnal sky had reddened and was ablaze with flames of crimson and gold. He couldn't ever recall the setting sun more salient, the mountains in the west, fading peaks set against an awesome firestorm. The evening sky was sublimely beautiful but there was also a strange foreboding present in the atmosphere, a terrible sense, he felt, of something pending and threatening, as though the world's catastrophic end was imminent.

Somewhat punch-drunk, he staggered his way back down through the village, to the lower road running parallel with the natural curve of the bay. His head was still a jumbled mess of confusion and all of his gumption had deserted him. Shuffling his feet and fidgeting with impatience, he again had a hankering to leave these shores. It was as though history was repeating itself and now he looked upon himself as an utter fool.

Twenty-five years ago he'd vowed never to return here and just like before he wanted desperately to flee the country. But he knew deep down that that just wasn't possible. There were still a few more days remaining of their holiday but if it wasn't for his wife's sake, he would have undoubtedly crossed the road and caught the bus travelling in the opposite direction, all the way down to Desenzano, where he could have taken the first train back to Paris, via Milan, and then another on to London.

Reluctantly, he got on board the tourist bus that would drive him back round to the other side of the bay, feeling gloomy and dejected and with inspector Leopardi following covertly in his wake.

20

The diligent inspector had continued to shadow him from the cemetery down to the lower road. He'd waited in his car for a short while before following the bus around the bay where it stopped outside the Maximillian Hotel. He pulled over onto the verge a short distance by the bus stop and gazed into his rear view mirror. Without bothering to turn off the ignition he sat and carefully observed his suspect, again studying his body language as he had patiently done for most of the afternoon. He saw him alight the bus appearing much distressed as he shuffled down to the hotel's entrance, his face strained and lost in thought, his shoulders hunched over like those of a wretched beast of burden.

What was it about this curious Englishman? he pondered. The inspector had spent the latter part of the morning metaphorically sniffing around the private grounds of the Machiavelli mansion, scratching at the surface, trying to tempt providence to throw him the bones of a clue in order to justify his own grim conjecture. So far he'd found no irrefutable evidence to back it up but was far from satisfied, that bloodhound nose of his having detected a scent all too familiar, the smell of trouble.

Yesterday, he'd merely mentioned the Machiavelli estate as a matter of course but then had done so again intentionally, trying to provoke a reaction by calling the Englishman's bluff. Which indeed is exactly what he'd reaped, triggering some kind of alarm bell in the guy's head.

Of course, he had no idea of the connection between this man and the Machiavelli family but something was definitely awry. Beneath the pinnacle his men had searched half the day and half the night looking for a corpse that didn't exist, the suicide, which it would now appear to be nothing more than a figment of this crazy man's imagination. The inspector was now inclined to believe that he'd been stabbing in the dark and it was more likely that his sergeant had surmised correctly after all. Enough of this nonsense! He decided. They'd all been looking in the wrong place. No more of this pretence, it was time to take a proper look inside the property, above the crag!

He drove on towards Malcesine, heading directly for the town hall where he wanted to procure a search warrant, as was his prerogative to do so at this late hour of the day. In due course he intended to take a good look around inside the old house itself. But now of course, he was looking for something quite different altogether.

21

Ralph headed straight for the cocktail bar where he rather abruptly demanded a double scotch on the rocks. He knocked back the liquor in one fell swoop, instantly benefitting from its intoxicating effect. Rather more civilly, he then asked for a repeat, before finding himself a comfortable chair out on the empty unlit terrace. Although he wasn't a great fan of whisky, it was just what he needed right now, the strong alcohol working its way fast through his system like some wonder drug, enabling him at last to relax his tense muscles.

Sat alone in the twilight slowly sipping his drink, he rolled the little girl's stone around between his fingers and thumb and began to put his thoughts into some kind of logical order.

Gradually gnawing away at the threads of his paranoia, he tried to make some sense out of the nonsensical but his head was so messed up he struggled to recall even what day it was. Fed up to the back teeth, he was pining for his wife's company and her aura of normality but he knew that she wasn't due to arrive for at least another half hour yet. In any case, what was he going to say to her? How could he possibly explain? In the light of what he'd seen, or more likely imagined, he couldn't bear to confide in her now.

He was worried about the upset it would undoubtedly cause her, she'd be frantic and how could he expect her to believe him anyway? How does one explain that they've seen a vision or a ghost? He fretted, fearing for his own sanity. This whole situation was plainly absurd. He was aware that neurotic people sometimes spoke to themselves, but this, this was just bloody ridiculous! Perhaps Sergeant Bellini had assumed correctly all along, maybe he had lost the plot. Or could it be just a simple case of too much sun? He pictured the phantom again, the hologram of his younger self, which he'd watched miraculously vanish into thin air. Never before had he believed in the black arts or anything else remotely connected to the paranormal, always remaining sceptical about such things.

Now it seemed almost anything was possible having had his mind ripped open to the contrary. 'Oh for goodness' sake!' he cursed, slowly shaking his head. 'What am I meant to do now?' he asked himself, he knew he should have taken more notice of his wife and readily blamed himself. Over the past six months or so, she'd warned him several times about the dangers of continually working long hours. And he'd being doing it for years! Was this really it then? He wondered. Had he now finally begun to come apart at the seams?

Soon he began to question his own intellect and indeed even his own belief systems. What he'd experienced earlier up in the chapel and the cemetery cannot possibly have been real, he reasoned with himself, trying his utmost to think rationally.

So what was it then? An old memory, like a flashback

maybe, that in some ludicrous fashion had manifested itself into the vivid apparition? Whatever it was, he was wholly convinced that it was all in his mind. It must be! There was no other possible explanation. The thing he'd seen, regardless of how real it had appeared, was purely inventive and nothing more than a reverie of folly, he thought, sub-consciously conjured up from some dark, mysterious part of his brain.

In any event, he'd firmly made up his mind not to breathe a word of it or else he suspected he'd no doubt soon find himself restrained by those men in the white coats. They'd shackle him in a straightjacket, he guessed, and most probably muzzle him as well, before incarcerating him in a padded cell somewhere out in the back of beyond and then forgetting he ever existed!

He gazed back out across the bay at the hills above the gleaming luminosity of Cassone, where the old, empty house stood invisible, camouflaged by the night. The first time he'd ventured here, he recalled, he hadn't known that that was where Giuseppe's family had lived and now he wished he'd never set eyes on the place at all. His nervous tension was at last beginning to decrease but he'd begun to feel groggy, his temperature he knew was a touch on a high side and he was afflicted with odd aches and pains as if he'd contracted a bad cold. He gulped down the remainder of his drink and went to the bar to order another. He was in the mood to get blind drunk and to hell with the consequences.

22

Grace Ashton kicked off her shoes, dropped her carrier bags and collapsed onto the bed alongside her husband. She was totally exhausted, having spent the last three hours on a jam-packed coach travelling back on the congested roads, after near on eight hours of traipsing up and down the narrow shopping lanes of Venice. 'Hello darling, I'm sorry I'm late, there was an accident or something, on the motorway.'

Ralph groaned himself awake.

'Would you mind love, if I skip dinner tonight?' she asked, between long tired yawns. 'I'm completely pooped, and all shopped out.'

Ralph had been dozing off the effects of the whisky and was pleased that she was finally here. He hadn't been able to make it back to the bar for that third drink, having suddenly felt the urge to be sick and had chosen wisely instead to stumble his way back to the room where he promptly spewed his guts up. 'That's fine by me love, I'm pretty well bushed myself,' he confessed, having also lost his appetite.

Oh, by the way, how are you feeling now? Have you been lying here in bed all day then, love?'

'Practically,' he lied, wishing if only he had. Now it was most definitely a case of the least she knew the better.

'Ah, my poor husband.'

'It must have been one of those twenty-four-hour things,' he fibbed, cautiously. 'I don't feel so bad now though, just tired. I've cleaned the bathroom up as best I could.'

'Never mind love, I'll do it in the morning before the maid arrives. I'm glad you feel a bit better.'

'How was your day? Did you all enjoy the city?'

'Oh yes, it's such an exhilarating place, isn't it,' she replied, reminiscing over her exciting time. They'd visited St Mark's Cathedral, the opera house, a glass blowing factory, and a museum and art gallery and even squeezed in a traditional gondola ride down the Grand Canal. 'But oh, so tiring,' she yawned, shortly before nodding off completely.

23

Ralph woke up in a cold sweat shaking in fear of something iniquitous. He'd been shouting out in his sleep. 'Where are you?' he'd cried, over and over again. It'd just turned three in the morning and this was the third time in as many hours that he'd suddenly sprung bolt upright in his recurring dream, on each occasion, unwittingly disrupting his wife from her own rest. Again she leant over and turned on the bedside lamp. 'Ralph, wake up love, you're having another bad dream.'

He mumbled things that didn't make any sense, which wasn't unusual; Ralph had suffered from sporadic nightmares ever since she'd known him. But his face, she noticed, was measled in beads of sweat and when she felt his forehead, she understood with much dismay that he was actually burning up with a fever. Quickly, she leapt out of bed and fetched him a fresh glass of cold water from the bathroom, before gently coaxing him into swallowing a couple of her paracetamol tablets in the hope of bringing down his temperature. Settling him back against the pillows she applied a face flannel soaked in cold water against his brow. Extremely tired but overwrought with worry, she tried her

best to stay awake and listened with concern to his inco-
herent muttering, none of which was she able to decipher
into any logical meaning.

Ralph felt himself falling down through the darkness,
back into the carnage of his beastly dream. Deep within
his delirium, he believed that he is conversing with his wife,
relating the heinous details of his nightmare.

*Now it has begun Grace, he says... It's broad daylight and I'm
alone in a small cemetery, where all of the occupants seemed
to have vacated their tombs. I say alone, because the residents
here are merely brittle old bones, skeletons, clothed in their
burial gowns, or in their Sunday best suits and frocks. They've
aroused an amusing image in my mind, love, a congregation
of redundant scarecrows and corpses with heads like hairy coco-
nuts, sitting on their own gravestones, taking the fresh air and
admiring the lovely view as innocuous as old age pensioners
relaxing at the seaside.*

*But no, I'm mistaken. One of these resurrected bird-scaring
zombies, isn't quite as dead as I'd first assumed. Or should I say
'undead', for it has just stood up twitching with life and it seems
positively annoyed by my intrusion. This one though, looks
more like a tailor's dummy than a distant cousin of Worzel
Gummidge. It's certainly got style, dressed smartly in a brand
new blue suit and wearing a tasty pair of shades across its shiny
grey skull. To my impending detriment, it appears to have taken
a grievous offence to my breach into its privacy and immediately begins to proceed in my direction. Only slowly at first,
plodding with stiffness, but it isn't too long before it's actually
sprinting towards me. All I'm concerned with right now is my
total avoidance of this atrocity. So naturally, I get the hell out
of there as fast as I can.*

Anyhow, the dream is playing out like a pre-recorded video tape, for I now find myself, as I knew I would be, running frantically through a great fern covered forest in which I am, by the way, still relentlessly pursued by the same angry mannequin in the trendy blue suit and sunglasses. Except now, he's been joined by a herd of vicious looking wild boar, a hundred or more snarling snouts all trotting my way. My limbs are aching something chronic with fatigue and are beginning to act like jelly but I dare not relent my progress for fear of being ripped apart. As luck would have it, I spot my one chance of escape. A tree, unique among thousands of others, its strong branches having grown out conveniently low to the ground, much like a ladder. I'm tiring fast and I can hear the hungry pack gaining on me. With not a moment to spare, I skitter up the rungs like a startled squirrel to the relative sanctuary above. With bated breath and my expeditiously beating heart almost burst, I cling on and watch as my blood thirsty hunters pass by below, all oblivious thank God, to the whereabouts of their exhausted prey. It seems I was wrong about the hogs though, for now I learn that they are in actual fact huge rats and for some obscure reason they all appear to be soaking wet.

Soon after, when I'm certain the coast is clear, I allow myself to drop safely to the ground. I'm alone once more but now stood contrastingly in the midst of a vast, open desert. Hostile and scorching hot. Endless dunes, like expanding ripples stretch out in every direction across the barren landscape. There is nothing else in sight except for an abandoned yacht which has run aground. But of course this doesn't make any sense at all, for where is the sea?

To my utter consternation, I notice the skeleton man again, the one in the smart blue suit. He's stood in the stern of the boat and although he hasn't any eyes, he's looking down at me with much disdain but he says nothing. Worryingly, I scan my immediate surroundings for any sign of the monster rodents. Thankfully there doesn't seem to be any. We are quite alone, so inherently my focus returns to the abomination. In one of his bony hands, he's holding aloft a glass of chilled champagne. In the other is a burning cigar. To the side of him I can see a small table upon which there's a crystal glass bucket. This is filled to the brim with sparkling ice cubes packed loosely around a fat bottle of Dom Perignon. My mouth feels as dry as the sand that engulfs me and my thirst is raging beyond belief. The odious bastard then slowly sips the cool, refreshing French wine and glares at me as if I'd wronged him in some despicable way. To torment me further, he spills the liquid in the glass overboard and then, in the same spiteful manner, empties the contents of the bottle as well, all the while remaining mute. I watch helplessly as the champagne seeps wastefully into the arid, dusty ground. It is I who now shows contempt, for his mental cruelty has infuriated me. To vent my anger I clumsily attempt to scale the side of the boat but no matter how high I try to leap in order to get at him, the deck remains frustratingly just beyond my reach. He's fully aware of this and taunts me further by blowing his cigar smoke down into my face. I am so livid and riled up, that I am suddenly possessed with a burning desire to kill him, regardless of the fact that he's dead already. But my situation remains disheartening, without water I shall die. Finally I collapse to my knees resigned to my inevitable demise.

Exposed to the merciless heat of the midday sun, it isn't long before I start to think that I'm slowly going mad. I begin to imagine the sight of fresh, clean water, bubbling up through the sand close by. Only a tiny amount but nevertheless there it is, gradually forming into a puddle. I figure that it's probably just a mirage and so try to ignore it with nonchalance.

But then the flow speedily begins to intensify. So much so,

that it's soon gushing out of the ground effusively, like a spouting geyser. With my hopes now raised beyond all expectation, I determine the fountain to be the real McCoy and not a trick of the mind as I'd first believed, for I can plainly feel a fine spray of water droplets tingling against the skin of my bare arms and face. Bouncing back to my feet, thankful with joy, I cup the palms of my hands together in an attempt to capture some of this precious, life saving water which I achieve easily and consume post-haste.

Choking with revulsion, I spit out the brackish water, realising once again that I am clearly done for. But then, just when I'm about to give up the ghost, I notice more and more of these columns of salt water shooting up all over the place. The desert, to my great surprise, gradually begins to flood.

Soon after, I'm wading through a metre or so of seawater towards my only lifeline, the yacht which has become afloat. Now, with relative ease, I manage to climb aboard the vessel but oddly enough I find no trace of the skeleton man. I am somewhat mystified as to why I should care but nonetheless I call out for him continuously, across the rolling waves of what is now a gigantic ocean. I close my tired eyes just for a fraction and suddenly find myself returned to the cemetery. And now my love, I fear it all begins once again…

24

Later that morning, Grace gently knocked on the door of their room. She'd been relaxing down in the reception lounge, browsing through the tabloids. 'Ralph, are you awake yet?'

Her husband had only just begun to stir from his slumber. 'Er...yeah, I'm just getting up now.'

'No need love, stay in bed.' She said, entering the room. 'I've brought the doctor to see you,' she informed him, hoping that he wouldn't be too cross. Her eyes were heavy with tiredness but she'd been too worried about him to have lain in herself. She'd asked the doctor, who had primarily been summoned to the hotel by the anxious parents of a sick child, if he wouldn't mind attending to her husband who was also feeling poorly.

She'd already divulged that he'd been unwell all day yesterday with an upset tummy and sickness and had been hallucinating during the night. However, inwardly she was more concerned about his mental state of health rather than his upset stomach and so she'd also made the doctor aware that, in her opinion, she feared he was on the brink of a nervous breakdown. Pulling back the drapes to let in the light, she said, 'Dr Borelli has kindly agreed to take a look at you, Ralph.'

'Now then *Signor* Ralph, your wife tells me that you've been in the doldrums of late. What exactly are your symptoms?' the physician asked. He had a large, round smiley face, heavy-jowled, and a thin horseshoe of greying hair around his otherwise bald head. His English seemed to Ralph about twenty years out of date, but Ralph was thankful that the doctor spoke English at all.

Ralph, now sitting up in bed, glowered at his wife. He was upset with her for having arranged the consultation behind his back. However, he replied civilly, 'I think there's a problem with my nerves, doctor. I can't seem to relax anymore, not properly anyway.'

'Do you feel sometimes a bit jumpy?'

Ralph nodded, 'Almost like I'm frightened of my own shadow. And I feel tense all of the time.'

'*Si*, some tension, and you have problems sleeping, I think.'

'I haven't been sleeping very well.'

'Right, let's take a proper look at you.' The physician took his patient's temperature before looking into his eyes, ears and mouth. 'I see, I would now like to feel your pulse and take your blood pressure if I may. Please roll up your pyjama sleeve.'

Whilst the physician concentrated on the blood pressure monitor, Ralph glanced over at his wife. She was sitting on the stool in front of the dressing table with her head bowed slightly. In the mirror he noticed her pensive expression and he suddenly felt penitent. He wasn't really angry with her. To the contrary, he actually felt relieved and was more annoyed with himself, for not having gone to see his own

GP months ago, like she'd suggested. He caught her glance and winked at her reflection in the glass. She smiled and turned round to face him properly. Having secretly made peace with his wife he quickly perked up and was glad that the doctor was helping him. Now in a more light hearted mood, he asked, 'Well, what's the verdict then doctor, am I going mad?'

'Mad?' the doctor chuckled. 'No, no, I think not,' he added cheerfully, before proceeding to blow some of his warm breath onto his stethoscope. 'Now I must listen to your breathing *Signor* Ralph. Please unbutton your top. Breathe in please... and out... and in.'

'So what do you think is wrong with me then?' Ralph asked, a little impatiently. This was after the physician had completed his examination and was beginning to pack away the various pieces of medical equipment back into his leather bag.

'Nervous exhaustion,' he answered. 'That's my diagnosis. Both your pulse rate and blood pressure are raised and your breathing pattern is a touch irregular. But I'm glad to say, nothing too serious. Nevertheless, I'm certain that all of your symptoms are stress related. And long term stress is not a good thing *Signor* Ralph. So it's important that you now allow yourself a reasonable amount of time to recoup, and I do mean to rest properly!'

Grace looked at her husband and silently pleaded with him to do as the doctor asked. Ralph knew exactly what she was thinking and was now inclined to agree with her.

'By the way, what is your occupation?' the physician asked.

'I'm an engineer, doctor. I work for a large British construction company but it's mostly paperwork nowadays.'

'Ah, *si*, paperwork, sometimes more stressful I think.' The physician continued, 'Maybe you should consider reducing your work load *Signor* Ralph. Meanwhile, I'm going to prescribe for you some mild tranquillisers. They will help to calm your nerves and hopefully help you to sleep better. I think when you get back to the UK it would be a good idea for you to visit your own surgery, they will no doubt, follow on with a similar course of treatment.'

'Yes I will... Umm, tell me doctor, this disorder of mine, could it of caused me to imagine things?'

The physician frowned slightly but then remembered what Mrs Ashton had told him about her husband's delirium.

'Weird stuff, that shouldn't really exist.'

'Possibly,' he replied. 'If you were feverish, a high temperature coupled with dehydration.'

Ralph pondered over yesterday's strange event but took some comfort from the doctor's prognosis.

'Thank you so much Dr Borelli,' Grace said. 'We're extremely grateful to you.'

'Yes, thank you doctor,' Ralph agreed. 'How do I?' he asked, referring to the physician's bill.

'It's OK *Signor* Ralph; I will leave my account at the reception desk which you can attend to tomorrow. Good morning to you both. *Arrivederci.*'

25

Having missed breakfast, Ralph and Grace decided to have an early lunch at the hotel itself. Light snacks were readily available from noon at the veranda bar beside the swimming pool. It was another very warm day and on their way down they noticed their friends already cooling off in the water.

'Hi Fiona, Hi Stuart,' Grace called out. 'We'll come and join you as soon as we've eaten,' she promised, before addressing her husband. 'That's if you don't mind, love.'

'No, of course not,' he agreed, cordially, 'why don't we stay here for the rest of the afternoon, shall we?' He was feeling a lot better now, having finally caught up with his sleep, but it was mainly the doctor's reassurance which had helped to improve his attitude.

Grace expressed a sigh of relief, 'I was hoping you'd say that, I feel absolutely knackered after yesterday.'

They sat down at one of the vacant tables available next to the bar and after stealing a quick glance at the limited menu, both opted for the Bolognese served with pasta and garlic bread. Ralph ordered their usual coffee lattes and a couple of cold lager beers.

'Hey you two, do you want a beer?'

'Oh yes please, Ralph,' replied both their friends, pretty much in unison. They were currently involved in some serious chilling out, floating around the pool, lying face down on their inflatable lilos.

'I'll tell you what,' Stuart said, a short time later after having gratefully quenched his thirst. 'Give me your beach towels and I'll go and reserve us some of those nicer, more comfortable loungers,' he added, as a friendly gesture. Taking a peek up at the sun, he said, 'It'll be busy here later, and you know what that party of Germans are like, if we're not careful they'll commandeer the lot!'

Fiona, with one ear tuned in, then hollered out from the pool, 'Get me one of those wide ones with the arms, would you dear.' She'd made this request without even bothering to raise her head up from the lilo.

'*Jawohl, mein fuhrer*!' he returned mockingly, pretending to click his heels together before saluting her like a serviceman to his superior officer.

After their friends had retired to their favourite spot at the other side of the pool, Grace asked Ralph if he'd manage to get any proper rest at all.

'Not much, I kept on waking up.'

Grace was on the verge of reminding him that he'd also kept *her* awake for half the night but she suppressed the thought. As always, her ardour was one of selflessness.

'I was having this same weird dream over and over again,' Ralph explained. 'I hope I didn't disturb you too much, love.'

'Umm, I guessed it was something like that,' she remarked. 'You were delirious, Ralph, talking in your sleep and uttering nonsense. She chuckled, 'At one point, you were even droning on about pigs and all sorts of daft stuff.'

Ralph raised his brow, 'Really?'

'Honestly, I stayed awake and listened to you for a long while; trying to piece together some of your words but it was like a mad jigsaw puzzle. I was so dog-tired though and must've nodded off.' She had neglected to inform him that in truth she'd spent most of the latter part of the night pacing up and down the room worrying about him.

Following lunch, Grace went over and joined their friends at the pool side while Ralph nipped back to the room to fetch her magazines and also something to occupy his own mind, a memoir by Laurie Lee, *As I Walked out One Midsummer Morning,* that his son, Geoffrey, had bought him last Christmas. Ralph needed a good book like this to help him relax and to take his mind off recent disturbing events. After much deliberation, he'd finally put all of the upsetting stuff down to his bad nerves and was now completely satisfied that none of it had actually been real. It must have been his mind playing silly tricks on him, he'd concluded, all due to abnormal stress levels. He believed he'd experienced what some people might describe as a bit of a funny turn and it had really frightened him. To prevent things developing into an even more serious problem, a nervous breakdown for example, henceforth he intended to do exactly what his wife and the doctor had advised. Therefore he remained determined to snatch as much rest as he possibly could on the last few days of his vacation. And when they'd got back to England, he swore to himself to set in motion some life changing factors that would eliminate his stress for good – reducing his working hours by at least fifty percent was his first priority!

On his way back to the pool, he bought another round of beers at the bar and carried them awkwardly over to his wife and friends.

'Oh well done, old chap,' Stuart applauded. 'I was just umming and ahhing over another one of those. My shout though, I believe.'

'You're welcome,' Ralph returned, genially. 'You can stump up for the next lot if you like. Cheers everyone!'

Relaxing in the sun with their wine and beers Grace, Fiona and Stuart were chatting about the highlights of their shared Venetian adventure. Ralph, unable to contribute much to the conversation, pretended instead to have been rather fed up yesterday, having been confined to barracks all day long and dictated to by the necessity of a nearby toilet.

By three in the afternoon the atmosphere had become what can only be described as boiling hot, their desultory conversations fading to silent indifference. The sunny half of the terrace was now completely deserted; most of the sunbathers congregating in small groups around the edge of the pool with their lower halves dipped beneath the cooling water. Whilst their skins had turned red and blotchy and their strength had been completely zapped their tempers had most definitely frayed.

Stuart and the two women were lolling around in the infinity pool whereas Ralph had preferred to stay put in the shade under the cypress trees. He remained engrossed in his new book. The story was about the extraordinary journey made by its author back in the mid thirties when as a young man he'd tramped from one end of Spain to the other, triumphing over adversity. A remarkable feat, considering he'd set out from his Cotswold village an epileptic, alone and penniless.

Later, when Ralph, deep in thought, happened to momentarily lift his head up away from his book he suddenly had reason to be alarmed. He'd recognised someone standing over near the steps that led down to the beach. 'Well stone the crows!' he sighed, as he felt his whole being gradually succumb to an invasion of dread. He blinked once or twice to focus his eyes properly, for he couldn't quite believe what they were seeing. 'It can't be!' he tried to induce himself, 'Not again!'

But his eyes had told no lies. There he was stood, the stalker. As brazen as ever and as usual, he was glaring directly at Ralph. It was indeed the arrogant young man from Verona. Like before he was wearing his flashy sunglasses and dressed in the same blue suit and black shiny winkle pickers.

An odd choice of attire for these modern times, Ralph thought. He recalled wearing something similar himself, but that was many years ago, way back in his heyday. However, more to the point, how on earth did he manage to track him down here, all the way from Juliet's balcony? He quizzed himself. There had to be literally thousands of inns and hotels strewn all over northern Italy, yet there he was again, Ralph registered, as large as life and about as welcome as a turd in the swimming pool!

Then he panicked. Could this man be from the police? A representative possibly, of the Malcesine force. No, of course not, what was he thinking? Their visit to the city of Verona, he recalled, was prior to the suicide. Well who the hell was he then?

The anonymous young man began to make subtle gestures as though trying to entice Ralph down onto the shore. Staring at him bluntly in one moment and down at the lake the next. Ralph wasn't at all happy about the situation but he understood that this was something he had no choice but to get to grips with. Slowly he got up out of his chair and announced quite calmly, 'I won't be long you lot, I'm off on my walk.'

'What, in this heat!' his wife exclaimed. She was submerged up to her neck in the water. 'Are you sure that's wise, Ralph?'

'Don't fuss love, I'll be all right. And besides, it'll be cooler down by the lake.' He placed his book on his wife's sun lounger for safe keeping before adding, 'Look after this for me please, darling.'

'Well at least take your hat and sunglasses with you then,' she insisted.

26

This guy had clearly stepped over the mark, thought Ralph, and now he'd made it very personal! Whether or not the fellow turned out to be amenable remained to be seen but whatever the consequences, he'd made up his mind to have it out with this cretin once and for all.

Without letting on to the others, he followed the stranger down the steep path and along the shore, upping his stride in a manoeuvre to gradually make up the lost ground. Despite his best efforts though, irrespective of how much he increased his speed, the man somehow constantly remained a good ten metres ahead of him. But Ralph, after only a short period of time, accepted this as some kind of imposed condition and duly followed at a more reasonable pace. If he was ever going to meet this elusive character then he supposed it could only happen under the man's own terms. But who was this weirdo? And where was he taking him?

Ralph hadn't had to wait long for his answer for he now understood that he was heading for the peninsular, a spike of dense woodland which jutted out in the shape of an arc approximately a hundred metres long, forming the western side of the bay. A little while later he saw the man disappear into the thicket at the far end of the beach and soon after Ralph had crept into the woods himself. The undercover of the canopy of leaves was a welcome break from the sweltering heat, except now there was a problem, he'd lost sight of the man altogether. However, as there seemed to be only one rough track leading through the brush, he could only presume that the man had gone ahead this way.

Almost immediately, Ralph began to tense up. There was something not quite right about this copse, he thought. All was strangely quiet, nothing moved, everywhere constant and unchanging. The concentrated layers of leafy, static foliage high above had helped to cool him down but simultaneously muffled him in a pocket of fearful silence, an uncomfortable stillness in which his ears could no longer detect the joyous cries of the many holidaymakers, whom were at play on the beach or active out on the lake.

Not even the flutter of a bird's wing could he hear or indeed any other sound to indicate the existence of the world outside. The only noises present were the sounds of his own rasping breath and the snap of every twig underfoot and it unnerved him. Apprehensively, he continued along the winding dirt track, aware of a strong sense of danger all around, his eyes darting in all directions and half-expecting the guy to leap out in front of him at any given moment.

But before he knew it, he'd reached the end of the trail and felt rather relieved to find himself back out in the open air again, where the terrain beneath his feet became rocky and slippery, gradually falling away beneath the lake. The man was standing upon a large, flat boulder just before the water's edge. He had his arms folded and was stood motionless as though he'd been turned into stone, like one of the marble statues Ralph had seen in Verona.

Ralph had halted at the narrow end of the spinney but remained in the shade under the overhanging branches, protecting him from the blistering heat. He was facing his adversary head on. The distance between them now was only minimal, three or four metres at the most. At last he'd got him cornered, he thought. There was nowhere else for the man to disappear to. This time though, Ralph promised himself not to lose his temper, to remain calm and composed throughout. Violence was no longer an option, but he needed some straight forward answers, fast! He fired the first of his questions directly at him, 'OK, so would you mind telling me what this is all about?'

The man's infuriating silence prevailed, which was hardly surprising for Ralph had never once heard him utter a sound. But one way or another he remained determined to have civil words with this fellow. He studied the stranger, inquisitively. Like before, when he'd first noticed him in the Colosseum, he felt that there was something vaguely familiar about him but again he struggled to define what exactly.

'Who are you?' Ralph continued, straining to recollect. 'What do you want with me?' It then occurred to him that perhaps the young man wasn't physically able to speak. 'What's the matter with you? Why don't you answer me? Can you not hear me? Can't you talk?'

Quite unexpectedly, the man started to laugh out loud like some raving lunatic. His deplorable attitude was intolerable but Ralph, mindful of his own self-control, quickly reined in his temper and held firm his position, ensuring that he kept a safe distance. Ralph's mental alarm bell had rung loud and clear and he felt is wise to caution himself, this bloke could easily be some kind of nutcase and probably was. And who knows, he agonized, he may well have concealed about his person, a deadly sharp knife; a gun even or some other lethal weapon. The man was certainly lacking something and didn't appear to be right in the head. The longer Ralph listened to him, the more he began to consider him a prime candidate for the village idiot! But then he could just as easily be a highly dangerous mental patient, he thought, escaped from an asylum.

The hysterical young man suddenly stopped laughing and instantly reverted to his former stance of stony silence, before proceeding slowly to wiggle his right hand index finger, balefully summoning Ralph to step forward and to come a little closer. Ralph already more than a tad concerned, mumbled through gritted teeth, 'Just forget it, mate!' Without taking his eyes off the man for a solitary second, whilst at the same time pointing at the ground, he shouted out, 'No way my friend, I intend on staying right here!'

Catching Ralph completely by surprise, the man suddenly spoke. 'No?' he snorted, somewhat offended by Ralph's refusal to co-operate. 'But you *will* come with me my friend,' he assured him, with a voice which sounded tinny and somehow distorted. 'Sooner or later, I can promise you that Ralph!' he added rather blasé, before turning about and strolling down into the lake fully clothed.

Astounded by this deranged individual's erratic behaviour, Ralph carefully monitored his progress until the water had reached up to his waist. Whatever was this fool up to, he wondered? But more alarmingly, how did the stranger know who he was? Once again, Ralph's paranoia reared its ugly head and roared aloud, taking full possession of his current thoughts. What was really happening here, he fretted? Was this all part of some broader conspiracy against him? Why was everyone trying to drive him raving mad?

Suddenly, the young man spun round in the water to face him once more. He stared at Ralph for a few moments in a rather demeaning way before casually removing his sunglasses and slipping them into the top pocket of his jacket. Then the penny finally dropped as Ralph, recoiling in disbelief, clearly recognised the man's facial features. Shocked by the revelation, he was forced to grab hold of the nearest tree branch in order to steady his balance. This was a huge blow to his confidence for it was now evident that the crazy person half submerged in the lake before him and the crying man he'd chased yesterday through the streets and alleyways of Cassone, were one and the same. It was himself again, the desperate twenty-two-year-old that had run away from this country all those years ago.

'*Arrivederci* my dear killer,' the young Ralph said, with a degree of sarcasm, before turning about and resuming his journey to the bottom of the lake, as if he'd suddenly been biologically equipped with a set of amphibious gills.

Ralph's head felt like it was about to explode. 'How can this be so?' He panicked, watching the man's last exhaled breath bubble up to the water's surface. 'What in God's name is happening to me?' It was all too fantastic to be true. He closed his eyes and prayed that it was just another one of his dreadful nightmares. But this was no dream, he now understood. This was really happening! After the guy had disappeared under the water altogether then so did everything else, when Ralph finally blacked out and collapsed to the ground.

27

'I can't imagine what has happened to him,' Grace sobbed. 'He only went for his usual walk this afternoon but now, unbelievably, he appears to have suffered some kind of melt-down. I'm really worried about him, doctor. I can't seem to get any sense out of him at all.' She was wearing a cream coloured evening dress, matching stilettos and a plain single string of complimenting pearls, they'd planned to eat out this evening with their friends, the Meadowbanks.

'Please *Signora*,' Dr Borelli said, trying to calm her down. 'Let me take another look at him.' The physician prodded Ralph lightly on the corner of his shoulder, 'Hello *Signor* Ralph, can you hear me speaking?'

But Ralph was dead to the world and hadn't the strength to respond.

'He came back here about half an hour ago,' Grace explained, dabbing her wet, puffy eyes with a tissue. 'Never said a word staggering through the doorway, at first I thought he'd been drinking – he was unsteady on his feet and he looked a bit pasty. But then, quite suddenly, he just passed out right in front of me. He looked to me as though he was traumatised, doctor. Also, I think he banged his head on the wall as he fell.'

This had all happened of course, before she'd rushed off down to the reception desk and implored them to call the doctor immediately, having experienced some difficulty getting through on the telephone in the room. Stuart and Fiona, dressed up to the nines, just happened to be there as well. They'd been waiting patiently for their friends to come down and join them. However, having been informed of the unfortunate circumstances, they'd insisted on staying with her until the doctor arrived. It was Stuart who had heaved Ralph up on to the bed and made him comfortable.

'Would you mind *Signora*, placing some of those seat cushions here at the end of the bed; I think we need to raise his feet to begin with. Right, now let's see what we've got?' The physician felt around Ralph's head before shining a small torch into each of his eyes. '*Si Signora*, your husband has quite a nasty bump on the side of his head. But concussion, I think not.' He then proceeded with a more thorough examination of his unconscious patient and a short while later said, 'Umm, I had suspected that he may have been in shock but his blood pressure, which is slightly raised, suggests otherwise. His pulse and temperature as well are much the same as they were this morning. Which, may I remind you *Signora*, were not too serious.'

The physician's observations had not really gone a long way in helping to relieve Grace's anxiety, even though they were relatively upbeat. She was still attending to the bits of mascara peppered around her red, baggy eyes. 'Will he be all right then doctor?' she asked, already silently blaming herself for dragging him out here in the first place.

'*Si Signora*, I think he should be fine if he rests,' the

physician replied, reassuringly. 'But he is generally not a very well man and I still hold with my original opinion. Your husband is mentally exhausted and I must warn you that if he doesn't rest himself properly, I'm afraid his condition may never improve. I could have him admitted to hospital for a few days if you prefer…'

However, before he'd had the chance to elucidate, Grace interrupted him, 'All no doctor, I'd much rather he stayed here.' Her level of concern had risen sharply.

'Well, I was about to add,' the physician continued, 'but I'm not certain if that would help matters much in the long run. *Signor* Ralph is, I think, too much of an anxious person. When do you and your husband go back to the UK?'

'Not until Sunday.'

'OK *Signora,* I'm now going to give *Signor* Ralph an injection.'

Once again, her worry intensified.

'There's no need to alarm yourself, it's merely a sedative to relax his mind and allow him to sleep properly, which is important for his recovery.'

Grace helped the physician gently remove Ralph's outer garments before tucking him in the bedclothes. 'I want you to make sure that he remains here for at least all of tomorrow,' he insisted. 'Have his meals brought here to the room, I don't want him to have to lift a finger for the next couple of days.'

'Yes, all right doctor, I will.'

'Let him rest now. He'll awake in his own good time. And when he does, he's probably going to have a bit of a headache.' Dr Borelli looked at his timepiece, it was about to turn eight. 'I'll come back and check on him again sometime tomorrow afternoon, I think. However, you must contact me the moment you notice any decline in his condition or indeed any new symptoms. Don't worry though, my apartment is fairly close by and I can be here in a matter of minutes, if need be.'

As the physician was about to take his leave, Grace asked, holding up the small bottle of pills that she'd collected earlier from the local chemist, 'Will he still need to take these, Dr Borelli?'

'*Si*, please continue with the tranquilisers as prescribed. No need to alter the dosage at this stage. Well, now I really must take my leave.'

'Thank you so much, once again I am extremely grateful, doctor.'

Smiling kindly, the physician replied, 'you are very welcome, *Signora*. And remember please, to notify me straight away of any change, *arrivaderci*.'

'Yes, goodbye Dr Borelli. And thank you.'

Because of the unfortunate circumstances surrounding Ralph's sudden illness, Stuart and Fiona Meadowbank had decided to spend the remainder of the evening down in the hotel's lounge bar. However, after noticing the doctor leaving the building, they'd both felt obliged to nip up and check on their friends, taking with them several large gin and tonics and a plate full of sandwiches.

28

When Ralph finally woke up late the following morning, his head was pounding and the inside of his mouth felt parched. Instinctively, he rubbed the bump on the side of his head and was mystified as to how the injury had come about. He wondered where his wife had gone, before suddenly noticing her curled up asleep under a blanket in the wicker chair. Why hadn't she slept in the bed, he panicked? Had they had an awful row? Reaching over for the glass of water on the bedside cabinet, he felt a sudden twinge behind his ear which caused him momentarily to wince in pain.

His wife then began to stir from her slumber, yawning and stretching. She was pleased to see him now sitting up in bed and asked how he was feeling.

'Morning love, well I must say, my head hurts like one almighty hangover,' Ralph complained, before gulping down the water. 'Had we been out on the razzle by any chance?'

'Chance would've been a fine thing,' she replied, on her way through to the bathroom. 'We didn't even make our dinner date, let alone that new nightclub which we were going to try. Don't you remember?'

'Well actually no, I don't.' He tried to recall his movements yesterday but his mind was a total blur. The last thing he could remember clearly was when he was following the man along the beach. Again he tried to unravel the uncertainty in his mind but this was as far as his memory would stretch.

'Here, take a couple of these painkillers for your head,' she advised. 'You bashed it on the wall last night when you fell over. Do you know, you were so completely out of it I had to ask Fiona and Stuart to help me get you up off of the floor?'

'I don't remember getting drunk.'

'As it happens you weren't, but you were certainly wobbling about like you'd had a few.'

Ralph swallowed the tablets. 'I guess I'd mucked it up for everyone then. Were Stuart and Fi very upset?'

'Quite the reverse, they'd been rather worried about you, Ralph.'

Ralph felt like an apology was in order, 'I'm sorry love.'

'It was gone seven and almost dark by the time you got back here. By the way, where had you been to for all of that time?'

Ralph strained his memory. 'Grace, I really can't remember… bloody hell, I can't remember anything!'

Grace quickly pushed her curiosity to one side and said, 'Calm down love, the doctor said you must rest.'

'The doctor, what doctor?'

'Dr Borelli, he came here to see you last night after you'd passed out.'

'I thought you said I'd fallen over, are you saying then that I'd fainted or something?'

'Collapsed more like. And you've been out cold ever since. To be fair though, he did give you a strong sedative.'

'Who did?'

'The doctor did of course, albeit intravenously, to help you relax properly. You seemed very distressed Ralph. Did something happen on your walk?'

Ralph daren't mention anything about the man who'd beckoned him down to the shore but racked his brains again for any inkling of where he might have taken him to. Holding his head between his hands he again shrieked in pain. 'Bleedin hell Grace, there's nothing there. My head feels like it's just an empty numbskull!'

'You've probably got a touch of amnesia as well then, Ralph – when you bashed your head, maybe. Try not to worry about it love, we'll mention it to the doctor this afternoon. But I'm sure it'll all come back to you later.' She said, trying to console him before quickly changing the subject and adding; 'Are you hungry, Ralph?'

'Famished, but I don't much feel like going down to the restaurant.'

'Well that's just as well,' she informed him, while picking up the telephone receiver beside the bed, 'because you're having your meals here today.'

'Who says?'

'The doctor says so!'

Once again, it was a very pleasant morning and so they'd decided to have their breakfast out on the balcony. The weather was much the same as usual, above them a hazy blue sky, criss-crossed by jet vapour trails evaporating under the rising sun. Grace had ordered some cereal for herself and a full English grill for her husband. Ralph commented, when he'd finished guzzling down what was left of the fresh orange juice, 'I really enjoyed that, Grace. And do you know I believe that long sleep's done me the power of good. I feel as right as ninepence now. What's on the agenda today then?'

'What do you mean?' she asked, not fully paying attention to what he was saying.

'Well, what have you got planned for today, is what I meant. I was thinking that maybe we ought to do what Stuart and Fiona did. Get out and see a bit of the local countryside, we'll be going home soon.'

Grace then suddenly understood the implication of what he was proposing. 'I'm sorry,' she hurled back at him, adamant in her resolve. 'But you're not going anywhere Ralph. We're both staying right here, today!'

'You *are* joking, love.'

'I am certainly not!' she retorted, putting her foot down at last.

Ralph's jaw dropped with disappointment, sighing at the thought of being cooped up in the room all day long and the predictable boredom.

'No, I'm sorry Ralph, but I've promised the doctor that you'll rest up today,' she continued. 'And besides, he's coming back here later on to check on your progress and he'll expect to find you lying in that bed!'

'But I don't feel like going to bed,' he whinged, resenting the rebuke.

'Look love, I'm just about at the end of my tether with all this worry,' she fired back, before bursting into another flood of tears.

Finally comprehending the extent of his wife's concern and succumbing to her emotional state, Ralph said softly,

'Let's not argue about it then, love. Please don't upset your-self. OK, OK I promise to do as I'm told today,' he agreed, holding up his arms in surrender. He then embraced her lovingly, 'But tomorrow Grace, we're out of here, agreed?' His wife, marginally relieved, nodded her approval of his compromise. At least she'd managed to pin him down for one day, she thought. It was a start.

The doctor's visit had merely culminated in a re-empha-sising of his previous advice and as regards to Ralph's mild memory loss, he was informed that it sometimes occurred with patients suffering with severe anxiety but was usually only temporary. The remainder of the day however, had turned out to be non-eventful. To help pass the time away, Ralph had attempted on more than one occasion to get back into his novel but his mind persistently refused him the luxury of concentration. Whilst his wife had been content to spend the rest of her day sunbathing out on the balcony, Ralph had lain on the bed, complaining to himself of weari-ness and apathy.

29

At the crack of dawn Ralph had noticed that the sky was rather murky but now, thankfully, it had turned much brighter and according to the weather forecast, things were expected to improve as the day progressed. After breakfast, they'd both decided to get up off of their backsides and do some exploring of the local area.

To begin with they visited the nearby Roman villa of Castelletto, one of the best preserved Roman edifices in Northern Italy, before sampling a glass or two of another local wine called Valpolicella, along the waterfront at Assenza. The next port of call was Limone, so called because of its famous lemon groves with their tall stone pillars stretching along the mountain terraces, via the port of Malcesine on the tourist ferry. Here they'd spent a delightful hour or so exploring the idyllic church and the charming narrow shopping lanes before returning on the same vessel, enjoying spectacular views of the lake and surrounding mountains and the superb thirteenth century Scaliger castle which dominates.

Walking up to the Monte Baldo cable car terminus, they passed by the bus depot where Ralph happened to notice the local police station tucked in behind. Regretfully, it put him in mind of the inspector and his uncouth sidekick, Sergeant Bellini, causing his heart to flutter when he started thinking involuntary about the suicide again.

Leopardi's men had combed the entire district and had found no evidence to support his claim of a person having committed suicide. This of course was only to be expected for Ralph was now convinced that he'd perceived it merely in his own mind. The man or ghost or whatever the apparition was meant to represent, was simply a product of his own imagination and nothing more. The 'Jesus Man', as the inspector had referred to him, who'd appeared to fall to a certain death, did not exist, he reassured himself. Nor did his naked friend from the olive grove, who he believed he'd chased across the fields and down the winding lane to Cassone into the little chapel with no name. He tried his best to shake away the demons, refusing them time to fester. As far as he was concerned these entities no longer held any credence and he was determined not to let the memory of them ruin his day.

But no sooner having found this new fortitude of mind, the world about him suddenly became unreal and incomprehensible. Again, he was upset and rattled. 'Oh hell it can't be,' he grumbled to himself. 'I don't think my nerves can take much more of this!'

He could have sworn that he had just seen the imposter again; his crazy lookalike from Verona, whose ability to breathe under water indefinitely now seemed an undisputable fact! Admittedly, it was only a brief glimpse, when the gondolas had passed each other half way up the side of the mountain. But he was positive it was him, standing alone in the opposite cable car, heading down. He was dressed exactly the same as before and as always, he was glaring back at him with the usual degree of deprecation. But hang on a moment, Ralph checked himself, had he really seen this man or was he just imagining things again? He shook his head with frustration in an attempt to clear away the maddening thoughts. Now he just didn't know what to believe, one way or another.

When they'd reached the 1800-metre summit of the mountain, Grace noticed that there was something terribly wrong with her husband. The colour had drained from his face, he looked grey and she feared he was about to pass out again.

'My God Ralph, you look awful.'

'Thanks!'

'No, I mean you don't look right. What's the matter with you? Are you feeling ill again?'

'Well actually, now you come to mention it, I do feel a bit woozy.'

Grace promptly ushered her wavering husband over to the row of wooden benches, she'd noticed leaning up against the side of the gondola sheds. 'Let's sit down here and rest for a bit,' she suggested, 'there's no hurry.'

This was the starting point of a well-trodden path which meandered for miles into the majestic snow-capped mountain range, awesome and wonderfully silent. They had planned to hike along part of the route but unfortunately, Ralph's sudden shortness of breath and debilitating dizziness had now put paid to that idea. Even so, Grace now felt like she was sitting on top of the world, the views of the lake and surrounding mountains were breathtaking; the empty sky all around was so perfectly blue and seemed to reach out as far as forever.

'It's all coming back to me now,' Ralph said, unable to withhold things any longer. 'The other day, at the pool, I'd noticed this cocky looking fella, he was standing over by the beach steps and he just kept on staring at me.'

'Fella, what fella?'

'The same moron that'd tailed us around Verona last week!' Ralph explained. 'I never told you about him at the time because I didn't want to alarm you.'

'Really, I don't remember anyone following us.'

'Yes well, you was too busy enjoying yourself love, and rightly so.'

Grace, keen for him to shed a bit more light on the matter, gently placed her arm around his back and carefully listened to what he had to say. 'Go on, love,' she said.

'Anyhow, the man that had stalked us around the city was definitely the same bloke who'd showed up at the pool. Do you know, it must've been ninety-odd degrees that day but, believe it or not, he was wearing a suit done up at the buttons – strange guy!'

Grace commented, 'I don't recall anyone dressed like that. And why had he followed us around Verona then? What did he want?'

'It beats me!' Ralph replied, shrugging his shoulders. 'I never got the chance to find out. He was worse than that Houdini fellow, one minute he was right in my face then in the next moment he'd completely vanished.'

'Didn't you find all of this a bit odd then, Ralph?' Grace asked, starting to worry a bit about what he was saying.

He was scathing, 'Of course I did, and at the time I felt like I wanted to punch his lights out!' He glanced at his wife and noticed that she was frowning at him. 'Well, he kept on gawking at me, like he was trying to wind me up.'

'What do you mean?'

'Purposely staring right into my eyes; the bastard was tormenting me, Grace. Do you know I was this much away from landing him one?' He added, forming a small gap between his index finger and thumb.

Grace frowned again and quivered apprehensively.

'Anyway, when he turned up again at the hotel I'd had just about as much as I could take. So unbeknown to you three, I got up and followed him down to the beach and along the shore. I was determined to find out exactly what his game was but by the time I'd reached the woods I'd lost sight of him altogether, mores the pity.'

'What did you do after that?'

'I carried on regardless, along the dirt track through the trees until I'd got to the far end of the peninsular. And that's where I found him again. Standing there, as brazen as you like, with his arms folded like one of my old schoolmasters waiting to reprimand me. I wanted to ask him what the bloody hell he was playing at but I could hardly believe it, the prat only walked down into the lake fully clothed, and then had the audacity to ask me to join him.'

Grace sniggered, half-heartedly, 'So what did you say?'

'Well it was obvious by then that the lad wasn't all there,' he replied, rotating a finger clockwise against his right side temple. 'So basically, I told him to get lost, but that's when I recognised him, Grace, after he'd took off his sunglasses.' Ralph paused for a moment, recalling the shock he'd felt, and that awful feeling stirring in the hollow of his stomach.

'Well, who was it then?'

Ralph hesitated… 'Me, it was me Grace, can you actually believe that? I was stood there staring at my own face!'

Grace sighed with relief but also with a sense of

helplessness. She tried to make him understand that he'd clearly been hallucinating again, possibly a side effect of the doctor's medicine, she suggested, supportively.

'Never, what in broad daylight!' Ralph exclaimed. 'He was as real as you Grace, let there be no mistake about that.'

Grace was almost in tears, she hadn't quite realised the extent of her husband's psychosis and wished they were back home again, living their humdrum lives. 'Ralph,' she sighed in desperation, leaning her head on his shoulder. 'What's happened to us?'

But Ralph went on as though she hadn't spoken, 'after he'd disappeared under the water though, I sort of came over all dizzy, it was the most awful feeling. I felt like I'd lost my bottle and I was really scared. In that moment Grace, I honestly thought I was going mad and I just wanted to run and hide somewhere. But then everything suddenly went black and that's when I suppose I must've flaked out. I'm not sure what happened after that, it's all still a bit of a mystery I'm afraid.'

'It sounds very much like you were having some form of extreme panic attack,' Grace remarked. 'But even so that doesn't mean you're going mad Ralph, a lot of people experience this type of thing at some point in their lives.'

Ralph was stooped forward, cradling his giddy head in the palms of his shaky hands. He just didn't know what to believe anymore. Grace finally stood up and said, 'Come on Ralph, I'm taking you back down to the village.'

A few minutes later they joined the queue of descending passengers and despondently hopped onto the next available cable car heading down.

30

The morning had begun mainly overcast but now that the clouds had finally dispersed, the temperature again was rapidly beginning to rise. Ralph and Grace Ashton had already taken shelter from the soaring heat and were seated in the shade under a leafy tilia tree in a picturesque *piazza* in the centre of the town.

At the highest point of the square, which gently sloped down towards the lake, there was a church that had its arched doors wedged wide open, welcoming its flock as well as the general public. Its façade, they noticed, boasted a number of fascinating gargoyles carved out of its stone buttresses, an exquisitely beautiful building, and noble among the parish.

Situated among the several restaurants crammed full with customers, there were several other busy establishments, including an ice cream parlour offering every flavour imaginable, a newsagent selling foreign tabloids and magazines, cheap cigarettes and souvenirs, and a little cupboard shop stuffed full with leather handbags, wallets and purses. Standing happily behind a colourful painted market stall barrow, there was a large Italian man wearing a chef's white hat and apron.

He was serving up generous slices of freshly baked pizza to a long queue of hungry holidaymakers whilst at the same time striving to emulate the vocal talents of his fellow countryman, the famous tenor, Luciano Pavarotti. A tall black man, adorned in a brightly coloured robe, had seized the opportunity to jump on the back of the bandwagon and was mingling among the charismatic singer's many admirers and fans of his delicious cuisine, trying to peddle his own merchandise, numerous trinkets, bangles and other items of cheap jewellery.

When the waiter fetched them their coffee lattes, Ralph became very anxious and was preoccupied with scrutinising each and every passerby, looking for the person he'd seen earlier that bore such a remarkable resemblance to himself as a young man.

Grace thought that he still looked gaunt and she was worried about him. 'I don't think you're quite yourself, are you love? You still look a bit peaky,' she commented. 'Shall we go back to the hotel after we've drunk these?'

'No, no, I'll be all right in a minute. I just felt queasy that was all. I could do with a stiff drink though,' he added, before summoning the waiter back.

'*Si, Signore.*'

'May I have a large gin and tonic my friend, *per favore.*'

Grace flashed him a disdainful look. She was also concerned about the amount of booze he'd been putting away lately.

'For my nerves!' he exclaimed, pre-empting any animosity she might have felt towards him. 'Would you like one?'

'No I don't!' she rebuffed, laconically, before having a

sudden change of heart, reconsidering that perhaps he ought to take a drink or two, it'll help to relax him. 'Oh go on then,' she said, more civilly. 'I'll have the same.'

A great hush panned out over the heaving crowds of tourists when a female Filipino busking violinist, pitched outside of the church, began to play Franz Schubert's *Ave Maria*. When the talented young musician had concluded the piece, they'd both noticed how several members of the older generation had been forced to dry their eyes before, all of a sudden, everyone in the square began to cheer and whistle. A honeymoon couple, in their mid-fifties, sat in the rear of an open top bridal tuk-tuk – complete with an appropriately dressed chauffeur, rolled slowly by. They'd just got married at the castle. The smiling bride, a gorgeous blonde all in white clutching a huge spray of lilies and roses; the delighted groom, dark headed and dressed in morning grey. They looked very much in love. Everyone, including Ralph and Grace, applauded and wished them well.

Later, after browsing round the shops through the bustling cobbled lanes, they refreshed themselves with a light snack at a pleasant open air restaurant down beside the port. Grace noticed, rather relieved, that some of the colour had returned to Ralph's cheeks and he was acting more like his old self. They shared a small pepperoni pizza, after which Ralph ordered himself another gin and tonic.

'Is that prudent, Ralph?' she remarked, dabbing at her greasy lips with a napkin. 'The tranquillizers, remember.'

He shrugged his shoulders. 'I doubt it Grace, but it's certainly making me feel better. Anyhow, a fat lot of good those bloody pills have done me! Would you like another drink?'

Grace hesitated, 'Oh to hell with it, go on then!' she

agreed, more cordially. 'I might as well go with the flow. But Ralph, you shouldn't discount the doctor's medicine so lightly, you haven't given them a chance to work properly yet.'

Ralph nodded, conceding her point. 'Cheers then, love!' His thoughts were now altogether more orderly and he was trying his best to forget all about the episode up on the mountain.

Sipping their ice-cooled alcoholic beverages, they sat back in the comfort of the shade, content to do as the Italians did and simply watched the world go by. Near the edge of the wharf they saw another busker wearing a black and white striped vest with an accordion playing some toe-tapping French folk music. Egged on by droves of fun loving pass-ersby, he nodded his gratitude each time they tossed their coins into his velvet beret placed on the pavement before him, and smiled at them as they danced to his tangos and waltzes, reliving their younger years. A little farther along, there was also a very clever mime artist with his face painted like a clown's, performing his silent act.

The sun in the cloudless sky had gradually arced its way round and was now burning down directly above them. They decided to leave in favour of a visit to the *Palazzo dei Capitani*, built in Venetian gothic style and located only a short walk along the waterfront. And it was while they were here that Ralph saw his doppelganger for the second time today. The young man was stood between two marble columns supporting the stone porch way to the rear of the building, leading out on to a pretty flowered courtyard in which they were stood admiring its beauty. He was sneering at Ralph in his usual derisive way.

Like a bolt out of the blue, the remainder of Ralph's

recent memory loss came rushing back to him. Without letting onto his wife in any form or fashion, he recalled how frightened he'd felt when he'd woken up in the pitch darkness at the nib of the peninsular. Disorientated and hardly able to see anything at all, he'd listened scrupulously for any sound of human activity but the only noise he heard was the constant barking of a tormented dog somewhere in the distance. Gradually piecing together a vague recollection of what had happened to him earlier, he'd soon become aware of his location. Forcing himself back up onto his feet, feeling rather light headed, he'd tried his best to blinker his fear while willing his weary body forward. Under the pale moonlight, he managed to retrace his steps back through the dark woods, pushing himself blindly along the trail until he'd reached the shore and in due course the hotel. He was glad that his memory had returned to him but considered it wiser if he didn't mention any of this to his wife for the time being. He believed he'd upset her enough already.

Whether it was the drowsy effect of the alcohol or his new logical approach to ghost spotting, he could not tell. All the same, on this particular occasion, he was a lot less troubled by the visage of his own spirit, if indeed that was what it was. But Ralph was now more inclined to think that he had nothing to fear from this young man, who just happened to remind him of himself from his earlier years. Granted, the juvenile clearly had an unhealthy interest in him, an obsession of some sort but God knows why? He thought. To test this adamant belief that the fellow was as human as himself and not the supernatural being he'd previously thought him to be, he decided to take a flutter on his own mental credibility. 'Hey Grace, take a look at that young man over there, standing on the steps.' He said quietly, whilst pointing with his eyes. 'Have you noticed him yet? Clock the way he's staring at me, anyone would think that I'd just pinched his wallet or something.' Ralph hadn't been that much older himself, when he'd first started courting Grace and he was wondering whether she'd recognise the similarity between himself and the stranger.

Grace was baffled. She was staring at the doorway directly behind him but there was nobody there. 'Who do you mean?' she whispered. 'What man, where?'

Ralph spun round and saw the tiresome young man as plainly as he could see his wife. 'That man over there, standing between the columns.'

'But there's nobody there, Ralph,' Grace replied, her eyes remaining fixed on the doorway.

Raising his brow, Ralph swung round once more just to be sure and he *was* still there, wearing the same scornful, contemptuous grin. Ralph had gambled on his own sanity but refused to accept defeat. For a split second he'd even begun to doubt his wife's loyalty, incensed by the thought that perhaps she was lying to him. Maybe all along she'd been in cahoots with everyone else involved in this conspiracy against him. But he looked at her and saw how contorted her facial expression had become with love and concern. He quickly banished the ridiculous notion as delusional rubbish.

'You really can't see him, can you?' He said, lowering his head in shame, suddenly feeling vulnerable and confused.

His wife silently shook her head.

'Then I'm clearly losing my mind, Grace,' he grimaced, holding his head in his trembling hands.

'You're not losing anything Ralph, or anyone,' she told him, feeling worn out and exasperated.

Believing himself to be tinkering somewhere on the periphery of madness, he began to admit his misgivings. 'I've just about had enough of this, Grace. I can't cope anymore!'

'You've been over doing it, that's all,' she continued, trying her utmost to reassure him. 'Why do you think I've been nagging you for months on end to take a proper holiday? You're totally stressed out love and this has got to stop right now! Whatever it is that's bothering you so much, you've got to let go of it, Ralph,' she shouted, embracing him tearfully and shaking with worry. 'Remember what the doctor had said, if you don't allow yourself sufficient time to rest properly then you're really going to make yourself seriously ill!'

Conforming to his wife's demands, Ralph dropped his shoulders, slowed his breathing and tried to put things back into perspective. Over her shoulder, he chanced another glance at the porch way and saw that the man had gone. But it wasn't really a man, he conceded. It was a lost spirit, an embodiment of his own guilt complex trying to control his mind.

Grace linked arms with her suffering spouse as they strolled down to the water's edge at the bottom of the courtyard, where the captains of yesteryear had once come ashore. His mood, she observed, had turned insipid. 'Don't worry love,' Grace said, 'I'm sure everything will be all right as soon as we get you back to Rochester. You'll be able to rest properly when we're home again, but you're not going back to work, Ralph. Not yet, not until you're properly better... I've a wonderful idea; let's take the long way back to the hotel, love. It's a nice walk down alongside the lake and it'll do us both good.'

To access the pedestrian pathway that hugged the side of

the lake, they first had to take a u-turn back through the village to negotiate the busy main highway. Before they could cross over it safely, an array of noisy Vespa scooters, weaving their way in and out of the local traffic, came thundering by.

Grace noticed a tanned young woman, wearing inappropriate high heels hugging a dark-haired, confident looking young man on a silver-chrome Lambretta. Ralph had noticed them too and also the fact that the biker with the rictus smile and not wearing a safety-helmet was the same young man he'd seen twice already today. It was the younger version of him again. And this time it was no coincidence, he thought, having now become attuned to the idea that this thing, whatever it was, was most definitely trying its hardest to drive him totally insane!

31

In silence, Ralph and Grace sauntered down the tree-lined avenue, towards the soothing blue water of the lake, under a continuous umbrella of shiny green and copper leaves. Ralph had hardly spoken a word since they'd departed Malcesine. To Grace, he seemed farther away than ever, his mood having become sullen and withdrawn, but she'd already decided that now was not the time to try to infringe on this private hell of his. However, as soon as she'd got him safely back home to England he was going straight to the doctors, even if it meant dragging him there herself.

The long walk had tired them both and as a consequence they were no longer in the mood for socialising. By the time they'd got back to the hotel they'd already mutually decided to forgo the formal dinner this evening, preferring instead to grab a couple of hotdogs each and a glass of ice-cold coke round at the beach burger bar. They were both in need of a good night's sleep.

Grace said, in a vain attempt to distract him from his depressive thoughts, 'As we're going home on Sunday, do you mind if we pop along to the market tomorrow? I'd like to buy some last minute presents and maybe a couple of souvenirs too.'

Shopping for mementos was the last thing Ralph wanted to do. 'Would it be all right if I just stayed here, Grace?' he asked, sounding broken and rather fatigued. He was past caring about such trivialities and was on the verge of giving up.

'Umm, yes of course, darling,' she responded, sympathetic to his mental state of mind. 'In any case, it'll probably be quicker if I went by myself.' Then she added, more enthusiastically, 'Maybe Fiona and Stuart would like to come along?'

They sat down on one of the iron benches facing the calm waters and ate their frankfurters and fried onions lined with mustard and ketchup. It was late in the afternoon when the shore usually settled back to an unspoilt peace and quiet. The temperature had dropped a few degrees and they were satisfied just to sit and wonder at the glistening surface of the deserted lake. It sparkled like a plateau of diamonds and sapphires and possessed a tranquillizing quality all of its own, guaranteed to cradle one's heart and enrich the soul.

After they'd eaten, Ralph began to stare intensively at his wife for he'd become deeply worried about her. 'Here, slip this into your purse Grace,' he said, handing her the shiny pebble which the child had given him.

'Oh, that's pretty,' she remarked, studying it closely. 'Where did you find this?'

Deflecting his wife's question, he said, 'Promise me Grace, that you'll always keep it by you,' almost resigned to the notion that he was somehow losing her. He knew damn well that he'd made a terrible mistake coming back to this place; to Val di Sogno, the Bay of Dreams and couldn't help

wondering that before he was able to leave it again something detrimental was going to happen, either to him or his
spouse and he prayed to God, that he'd once held close to
his heart, that nothing untoward should happen to Grace.

'What do you mean, like a kind of talisman?' she asked,
still admiring the fascinating markings on the stone.

'Look, just promise me, Grace!' he pleaded. She could tell
that he was very sincere but had also detected his growing
irritation. 'Keep it!' he added, 'It's just something for luck!'

'All right, I promise, Ralph!' she fired back, in the hope of
appeasing him and noticed straight away the relief written
all over his face. She examined the pebble again with a fresh
curiosity, shook her head no more the wiser before popping
it into her purse for safe keeping. Ralph, lost in thought,
gazed around impassively but vaguely hoped that he might
soon see a butterfly or even a ladybird.

32

Earlier that same day, Inspector Leopardi had successfully received his official permission from the mayor's office in the town hall, to search the mansion on the grounds of the reasonable explanation he'd put forward; namely, a suspect at long last for the possible unsolved murder of the Machiavelli boy. He'd been entrusted with the keys to the property by the real estate agents, whom had been appointed as caretakers, their contract with the Machiavelli family seemingly suspended in a state of perpetuity. Armed only with the official warrant and his flashlight, he'd gone there with one purpose in mind, to try and discover any possible link between the dead lad and the Englishman, *Signor* Ralph Ashton.

Having assumed correctly, he found that the electricity supply to the vacant property had been disconnected. As a consequence of all the windows being locked and permanently shuttered, it was of course very dark inside. In addition to this obvious hazard, he senses were at once repelled by an unpleasant odour lurking within its cold and unwelcoming walls, a potent smell of musk and damp. However, disregarding these minor pitfalls and with the aid of the torch, he set about his business and began methodically searching the mansion, room by room. The inspector was as sceptical as they come, but even he had to admit that there was something eerily strange about this sad, old place. It was a dead house, lifeless and as silent as its former occupant's graves.

The main living-areas on the ground floor were occupied mostly by a lot of antiquated items of furniture. Some of the pieces, including a grand piano, were shrouded in plain white sheets, whereas other possessions which hadn't been protected were cocooned in cobwebs. There were several oil paintings accompanied by a few stuffed animal heads and tapestries filling the wood panelled walls and locked away, displayed behind glass door cabinets, were family heirlooms and valuable items of crockery and silverware.

An array of pretty ornaments, vases and family photographs in fancy frames, all coated in a thick layer of dust, crammed the mantelpieces and the wall shelves and there was even a small amount of cash, he noticed, a couple of decommissioned lira banknotes weighted down by a ceramic figurine. Practically in every room priceless chandeliers hung dormant from highly decorative ceilings, and under his feet there were Persian rugs aplenty. But amidst all of these riches, that held the private memories of a family annihilated through tragic circumstances, there was nothing to connect any association whatsoever between to two men in question.

Undeterred, the inspector then began to snoop about in each of the bed chambers leading from off the top of the landing. He'd found nothing out of the ordinary among the endless wealth, evident at every turn and in every nook, but in the very last bedroom he eventually discovered something which promptly lifted his mood to one of optimism, when he'd spotted in the beam of torchlight a single black and white photograph. It was tucked loosely in the inside leaf of a paperback book lying in the top draw of a bedside cabinet, an old-fashioned Polaroid snapshot of the young Giuseppe, taken not long before he was killed, he guessed, grinning with his arm wrapped around the shoulders of another young man smiling.

They seemed happy in each other's company, vibrant and full of zest but what particularly interested the inspector was the notion that the second guy in the picture snap could almost be the young *Signor* Ralph Ashton, and the longer he studied it the more he became convinced. He, as well, began to grin with a certain amount of exultancy for at last he had found something tangible to show for his obstinacy and perseverance.

The photograph by its self was by no means incriminating evidence but at least it proved his hunch correct. The Englishman, at the time of the young man's death, *had* been his associate. He could tell by the look on their faces in the picture that they'd also been very close friends.

The astute policeman then suddenly recognised the print itself. He realised it was the very same photograph that had originally been circulated among the dead man's friends and acquaintances during the former investigation. Surprisingly, at the time, no one had been able to put a name to the anonymous young man or provide any clue to his identity. Not a single one of the interviewees had ever seen this stranger and to all intents and purposes he could just as easily have been another one of Giuseppe's numerous casual lovers.

33

The following morning, the penultimate day of their holiday, after Grace, Stuart and Fiona had caught the bus to the Saturday market in Malcesine, Ralph decided to take one last leisurely stroll along the deserted beach to get some fresh air. He hadn't slept very well and had a bit of a headache.

Last night, after heavy black cloud had drifted in from the west, the temperature had dropped dramatically for the first time in almost two weeks. It had rained quite considerably, gales sweeping across the land, gusts howling and moaning, and there had been television and newspaper reports of major storm damage up and down the country.

At one point during the night, Ralph had even felt the hotel itself shaking in its very foundations but all that remained of the hurricane was a light touch of drizzle, the cloud formations gradually thinning and resembling the rippled effect created by the tide receding out of a sandy cove.

Unusually, apart from one or two of the locals walking their dogs, the shore was completely devoid of any activity, as the sun shone inconspicuously behind a pearl-grey sky. But even in the absence of sunshine the lake remained enchanting and unprecedented, thought Ralph, its surface mist gently rising, thickening the silence beneath the desolate layer of calmness which had engulfed it, its inertia reminding him of the peaceful and wonderful time he'd once spent with his family up beside Loch Linnhe in Bonnie Scotland. However, as pleasant as it was, he knew he'd never be able to return here again, that was for certain. Despite this, he couldn't deny that it was probably the most tranquil place he had ever visited.

Consciously unaware of his movements, Ralph was surprised to learn that he'd actually wandered all the way round the bay to Cassone. It was no wonder his mind had been so easily distracted, he thought, what with all the upset over the past few days. He'd been thinking, what if the haunting should continue back home in England? What if he was never able to escape this thing? Soon he came before a small restaurant on the outskirts of the village where he noticed that all of the tablecloths had been laid for use but the place was in dire need of customers. He sat down at one of the outside dining tables by the rhododendrons and waited for somebody to come and serve him.

Glancing up at the hillside, he suddenly felt drawn by some strange, manipulative presence – something overpowering coming from up there again, he thought, directly above the shear face rock. It was almost as though the old house itself was trying to entice him back to the mountain. He tried to stay focused but it felt like the phenomenon was literally pulling his mind out of his brains, some nefarious, hostile beast trying to claw him back to the past. But Ralph was having none of it and instantaneously heaved himself back into the here and now. He ordered a coffee and gazed back across the lake in despair of the unknown.

For the next few minutes he was beside himself and struggled desperately to ignore the panicky feeling that had clasped his already fragile nerves. But no matter how hard he tried he couldn't make it go away, this curious sense of unfinished business. There was something evil up there all right; he was convinced of it, some overwhelming force; an entity that was slowly chiselling away at his weakening resistance and robbing him of every ounce of his will power. Inexorably, his opposition started to crumble and he began to persuade his wavering conscience that it was simply inconceivable that he should leave the country just yet, not until he'd had a chance at least to contend with this unknown malevolent thing. Whatever the cost, it all had to end here and now, he thought gloomily. There was no other way or else he'd never be rid of its imminent threat, permanently hanging over him like a black cloud.

It'd stopped raining, he noticed, and the sun had already begun to burn its way through the remaining mist. He paid for his coffee, which he hadn't even bothered to taste, and impetuously began to retrace his steps along the same route he'd trudged before. Up through the sleepy village again and beyond, continuing on doggedly, peering up at the old house each time it came into view, as the road snaked around the hills. He thought about his wife and was glad that she had accepted the little girl's pebble. Something told him that it would always protect her, a good luck charm. Steadfastly and rather recklessly, he forged ahead with this fresh resolve at the forefront of his mind, impervious to the distress the hike had caused him previously. He was determined to destroy this thing once and for all.

34

Meanwhile, at the headquarters of the police, inspector Leopardi was sitting alone at his desk waiting patiently for his assistant to arrive. His current rank and untarnished record in the force had earned him the right to his own spacious office, a large, glass partitioned area of the criminal investigation department. It was situated on the top floor of the building and looked down out over the whole town with the picturesque backdrop of the lake and mountains beyond. Officially, today was Sergeant Bellini's Saturday off and so the inspector reckoned he was entitled to be a little late.

But no matter because this morning the inspector felt in high spirits and was in no particular hurry anyway. He got up and poured himself another steaming hot cup of coffee from the dispenser before lighting himself one of his extra special cigars. These he kept locked away in the top drawer of his filing cabinet, reserved for such prestigious times like today that he knew would almost certainly merit. He was in a celebratory mood having last night received an important facsimile that he'd been rather hoping for from the passport and immigration authorities.

Recording each and every individual's entry and departure, back in those days, was of course simply impractical for any international border control. However, as a matter of standard procedure, occasionally certain situations did warrant special practices and therefore, in the interest of national security, the recording of personal information was deemed appropriate. One such incident, in the middle of autumn 1990, at one of the Italian-Swiss border crossings, had indeed resulted in the noting of certain details regarding the temporary detainments of a number of rowdy European youths, following a minor skirmish relating to a disruptive argument over their positions in the exit queues. Puffing on his expensive cigar, the inspector grinned with a certain amount of satisfaction for he had by chance, albeit by way of his own intuition, discovered his suspect's name firmly planted among the authority's list of troublemakers.

His hunch about *Signor* Ashton had paid off. He now had a date and a time. The photograph he'd found while rummaging through the deceased's belongings practically implied that the two men were known to each other, and coupled with this, he was now in receipt of a document that proved the Englishman had visited Italy once before, when only a young man of twenty-two. He'd stayed in the country for a little over two months but more to the point had suddenly departed again, crossing the border into Switzerland less than twenty-four hours before the naked body of Giuseppe Machiavelli had been washed up on the shores of Lake Garda. This, in the inspector's opinion, was no coincidence and was now almost certain that the Englishman had been involved in the young man's death. Clearly there were grounds for further investigation.

A local businesswoman, who'd been walking her dog

early in the morning, had reported the discovery of a naked young male, presumably drowned, washed up on the rocks just below the lakeside town of Castelletto. The inspector could remember the incident quite vividly, having been on duty that same day. He recalled, it hadn't taken his colleagues very long to discover the identity of the corpse, the man had been instantly recognised by one of the other young officers present at the scene. According to the coroner's findings, he'd suffered a blow to his skull through means incomprehensible to the court of inquiry but death had occurred as a result of drowning and consequently an open verdict was recorded. The police enquiries, which had involved interviewing scores of young people whom were known to be friends or acquaintances of the deceased, had by all reckoning, proved fruitless. In common with the vast majority of the interviewee's remarks was the claim that Giuseppe had, for the last couple of months leading up to his death, socially vanished, dropped right out of the scene as many had described. Unfortunately none of these people were ever able to give an account as to why this was so. Only through one or two of his close friends had the police learnt of his sexuality and ironically, also the fact that he'd actually been a strong and competent swimmer.

The mystery of the drowned man had seemed impossible to solve. But now, at long last, there seemed to be a speck of light at the end of the tunnel, a breakthrough after all these years in the dark. However, this development in the case was something Giuseppe's parents would never be able to thank him for, for his father had suddenly collapsed and died of a major stroke only a few days succeeding the tragic event. His mother, having slipped into a severe depression following the loss of her entire family, had attempted several times to take her own life. She was eventually sectioned under the mental health law and remains to this day, basically incarcerated in an institution for the mentally ill in Milan.

The inspector was fully aware of the fact that the English couple were scheduled to depart his country tomorrow evening by way of British Airways, via Verona airport. It was his intention however, and solemn duty to arrest *Signor* Ralph Ashton later this morning in connection with the death of Giuseppe Machiavelli. And to this objective, he felt very pleased and proud, now that he was so tantalizingly close to solving the riddle.

Nevertheless, there was still one part of this case which eluded common sense. He had yet to fathom out exactly why this eccentric Englishman had deemed it necessary to fabricate such a cock and bull story about a *nackid* man falling off the roof of the Machiavelli villa. He could apply none of his policeman's logic as to its significance, even though initially he would have laid a fair wager that the guy had been telling the truth.

'Ah, just the man I need,' the inspector said, as his assistant entered the office. As well as admitting that he'd clearly been wrong, he had something else to confide in him. 'It seems I owe you an apology Bellini, I think you were right about our foreign friend.'

The sergeant, having spent the night out on the tiles, helped himself to a cup of strong, black coffee. 'About the body, do you mean, sir?' he asked, his voice sounding hoarse.

'Yes,' his boss confirmed. 'Or shall we say about the lack of one. Anyhow, I'm now beginning to believe that all of that nonsense was just a smokescreen of sorts. Take a look at this would you please,' he added, passing his colleague a cardboard file, frayed around the edges and thick with papers. On top of the file he placed the photograph of the two young men accompanied by the facsimile he'd received yesterday evening.

'What is it?'

'It's an unsolved case from way back in the nineties, something I've been dabbling into of late.' The sergeant gave a perfunctory nod. 'Take a good look through it would you and tell me what you think.'

'What now, sir?' the sergeant asked, slightly daunted by the prospect. He was feeling rather hung-over and could think of better things to do with his time.

'Yes, but take your time about it. I've got to pop out for a while but I shouldn't be any longer than an hour or so, we'll discuss it when I get back. Pay particular attention, will you, to the unknown man in the snapshot.' The inspector stubbed out the remains of his cigar and left his suffering assistant to it. Unimpressed and yawning with tiredness, the sergeant opened the file and removed the top document. Reluctantly, he settled down and began to read the text.

When the inspector returned, he put his shopping to one side and helped himself to another of his favourite cigars. He offered one to his sergeant, who in his absence had become engrossed in the paperwork. 'Well, what do you reckon?' he asked.

'Interesting sir, but it's all still only circumstantial.'

'Yes, I agree, but do you remember how aggitated he became when I accidentally mentioned the property's owner? That seemed to imply that he hadn't actually known this beforehand and judging by his immediate reaction, it was plainly obvious that he was aware of something about the Machiavelli family.'

Studying the black and white photograph, the sergeant

lit his cigar, before commenting, 'And you think this other guy's the Englishman then?'

'I'd stake my reputation on it.'

The sergeant pressed his lips together and nodded his head slightly, 'Yes, I can see the resemblance, but what I don't understand is, is why return then to the alleged scene of the crime? And if he's come back here on some kind of guilt trip what was the point of concocting such a ludicrous story about the suicide? Surely, it would've been much simpler just to hand himself in at the station. Why bother sending us all on a wild goose chase?'

'Why indeed?'

35

This was the second time this week that Ralph had climbed these hills and having worked himself up into a lather of sweat, his bones and joints ached accordingly. However, at last he'd reached his objective and, panting with exhaustion, he peered up at the grand entrance to the Machiavelli estate. In front of him was a huge pair of wrought-iron, spiked gates painted black and tipped with gold metallic paint which, unfortunately, he soon discovered to be locked with a large padlock and chain.

Towering either side of the gates were twin brick built pillars, each crowned with a stone lion's head, spotted with rusty-yellow lichen, that tapered down to a two metre close panel security fence. A signboard that had been screw fixed to one of the columns read, *Proprieta Privata*. A short distance along the boundary however, on the left hand side, he noticed the fence had fallen into disrepair. At this point he was easily able to clamber through a wide gap in the broken panels and finally step foot onto the estate.

The grounds on this side of the barrier were a sorry sight indeed, he thought. Its landscape had been left to go rack and ruin, every tree, bush and plant growing wildly out of control and in the process of being choked by gorse and brambles and swamped by stinging nettles. But after only a short stroll along the gravel driveway, which had practically grassed over as well, he finally saw the great yellow mansion looming ahead. He halted for a moment. He guessed that once upon a time the old house would have been fit for a prince, but now it just looked terribly sad, lonely and forsaken. The weed infested driveway expanded into a circular forecourt in the centre of which was a stone fountain, complete with marble statues of cherubs and angels. It was dirty and defunct and smothered in wild undergrowth; the pool encircling it was full of dried mud. Situated intermediately around the curbed fringe of the forecourt were several more statues of the old Roman elite, marble centurions, emperors and Goddesses. His throat felt parched and he cursed himself for not having fetched a bottle of water with him. It was getting hotter as the sun climbed higher still in the cotton bud sky.

The house had a lot of windows, all of which had been shuttered and locked. The white paintwork on the slats had all but peeled away, the wooden frames, worm-ridden, damp and mouldy and lending weight to its overall shabby appearance. The main door beneath the porch was in much the same condition and the marble steps leading up to it were stained and pitted and there was moss growing up through the joins. Hastily, he tried the door knob, wondering tentatively if there was anywhere inside he could find something to drink, but found it to be securely locked as one would expect.

However, after a quick snoop around, he noticed a pathway of sorts which ran down the near side of the house. It led him around to the rear of the property where he was immediately confronted by a mass of jungle-like vines cascading down from the guttering, concealing the back of the house behind a thick green curtain of vegetation. There was no way of gaining entrance through this lot, he thought, not without the help of a machete. Slowly beginning to lose heart, he listened to the mystifying silence filling the courtyard and immediately felt himself to be almost floating upon it, as if his soul had prematurely escaped him, radiating outwardly.

He recalled having experienced something of this nature already, at those times when he'd been in close proximity to the young man, in the nameless chapel for instance, and when he was up in the cemetery and along at the tip of the peninsular. But the curious sense of weightlessness he felt on this occasion was somewhat short-lived when the song-burst of a startled blackbird taking to flight, caused him unexpectedly to leap up into the air almost abandoning his own skin. However, although his heart was still vigorously pumping spurts of fear, he'd finally found what he'd been searching for.

The spirit had been sat waiting for him on the steps of the iron fire escape affixed to the adjacent wall and evidently, in the meantime, had decided in his infinite wisdom to remove every shred of his clothing. His clothes were heaped up in an untidy pile before his bare feet. To Ralph, he now seemed to possess a strange aura about him, a kind of glow that could only possibly exist, he thought, between the parallel worlds of the living and the dead.

He wasn't sure as to the reason why but he'd suddenly become mindful of that terrible nightmare, the one that has continually plagued him following his daring escape from this country back in his youth; the one in which he sees the Devil whose face is the spitting image of his own.

He had come to look upon these regular sleep disturbances merely as nomadic memories lost in the desert of night, that strange domain of dreams and shadows. But he'd lost count of the amount of times he'd tried to analyse this particular nightmare which has never failed to disturb him. It was the one dream that he'd always worried about, often wondering about its meaning and its significance. But now, for some unaccountable inducement, he understood perfectly as he saw the whole, disastrous truth unravel before his eyes; the despicable truth that he's always refused to acknowledge and accept since that dark, lonely night sat on the shore when after a great deal of soul-searching he'd finally judged himself above reproach and innocent of any wrongdoing. And of course this was the real reason why he had never told his wife, having buried the reality of his misguided conception long ago somewhere deep in the folds and contours of his confused subconscious mind.

Only now, after all these years passed, was he overcome with such a sickening remorsefulness for the wicked deed he had committed. If only he were able to atone for his past mistake and wipe the slate clean, he thought, regretfully. To somehow travel back through time and alter the course of history in the desperate hope of exonerating himself. But what is done is done.

On that distant, shadowy night, when he'd so callously smashed his friend's head hard up against the keel of his father's yacht in a fit of guilt-ridden rage and contorted retribution, only a short while after the tycoon's son had attempted to sexually assault him. With all his strength and fury, derived from his temporary insanity, he'd held

Giuseppe fast under the cold, dark water until he'd dispossessed him of every choking breath of his privileged life. Only now did Ralph see himself for the murderer he was!

'You certainly took your time,' the spirit said. 'I was beginning to think that you'd never show up,' he added with a certain mordacity. Ralph couldn't help noticing that the skin on his face had thinned and had become taut, giving him an almost skeletal appearance.

He looked at his watch and saw that it was almost noon. Suddenly something clicked back into gear inside his head and, without a shadow of a doubt; he knew exactly what he had to do. Pooh-poohing the spirit's remarks, he barged passed him and hastily ascended the flight of rusty metal stairs. When he'd reached the very top of the stairwell, he noticed that the spirit was already there ahead of him, waiting on the flat section of the roof. Not particularly bothered or surprised by this, he rolled his eyes upwards faintly aloof before making his way over to the roof's perimeter where he calmly undressed and waited for the church bells to begin to toll.

36

Grace was delighted with her latest acquisitions, which she'd spread out all over the bed. Ignoring them temporarily, she went to rendezvous with her husband out on the sun terrace. Not quite expecting him yet, she ordered a glass of ice-cold cola and made herself comfortable in a cushioned chair underneath a canvas parasol. She was thinking about her children and friends back home and was looking forward to seeing them all again soon, especially Melissa, her pregnant daughter, for she was excited at the prospect of becoming a grandparent next year and couldn't wait to find out whether it was to be a boy or a girl.

Guessing that her husband had probably gone for another one of his long walks, she hoped he hadn't strayed too far. Still deeply worried about him, she'd noticed how much he'd aged in the past few days and how haggard he looked.

However, sidetracking her concerns for a moment, she almost choked on her drink when she noticed the man on the roof. She simply couldn't believe her eyes. It was like watching a tape recording of what her husband had already described to the police earlier in the week. As before, the man was completely naked and seemed to be preparing to leap off the roof of the very same building across the bay. Not quite knowing what to do for the best, she grabbed the arm of a nearby guest and pointed out the bizarre scene. Before long she'd enticed a whole crowd of people to possibly bear witness to the sad event, including the barman, a room maid, the pool attendant and the gardener. A little exhausted by her frantic efforts, she glanced down at her watch and mumbled under her breathe, somewhat niggled, 'Oh, where are you Ralph? If only he was here to see this for himself.'

Stuart and Fiona Meadowbank then showed up on the terrace wearing their swimming costumes and flip flops and carrying their beach towels rolled-up under their arms. Moments later they all heard the peal of church bells resounding from across the water and everyone fell apprehensively silent. They were joined by inspector Leopardi and Sergeant Bellini, whom had arrived with the incumbent task of arresting *Signor* Ralph Ashton.

But before the officers had even uttered a word, Grace had already cried out, 'Look inspector, over there,' she pointed, 'on the roof again!' She'd said it in front of her friends, almost gloating.

'Oh, my word, Stuart,' Fiona Meadowbank gasped. 'It's another one of those bungee jumpers in the buff.' She informed him, before scuttling over to the far railings hoping to get a better look.

Stuart Meadowbank, dawdling along behind her, exclaimed rather righteously, 'Well, it's probably just another student pulling a fast one. Exactly what I told everyone in the first place, you'll see!'

The inspector had been about to ask Mrs Ashton the whereabouts of her husband, but even without the aid of his binoculars, he knew that he was now looking at him. 'Get on the phone, Bellini; we better get the boys back over there fast.' He said, stern-faced and knowing full well that they were already too late. Like everyone else on the terrace, whom were standing poised and silent, he gazed helplessly over at the Machiavelli place across the bay with growing despondency and braced himself for the worst.

37

The spectre of his younger self, that had constantly haunted him since his return to Italy, effortlessly stepped back into Ralph's naked, trembling body and they again became one.

After the last bell had fallen silent, he heard a familiar voice inside of his head say, 'Come on then Ralph, if you're coming.'

Resigned to his inevitable fate, Ralph duly adopted the same pose as the suicide that he'd seen in the premonition of his own death only a matter of days before. Inhaling one last breath and tearfully trying not to think of his wife and children, whom he knew he would never see again, he then stepped over the confines of the roof and let himself silently drop over the edge into that other world.

38

An elderly Cassonian farmhand, who'd been attending to his olive trees, was the first person to arrive at the tragic scene. The horrific sight of the suicide's bloodstained body had forced the old man's hand over his mouth in an effort to prevent him from heaving up the contents of his stomach. The naked man was lying twisted and motionless on the sharp rocks like a sack of broken bones, battered and largely cut to pieces. The olive picker respectfully covered the torso with his work's apron before rushing off to raise the alarm at a nearby farmhouse. Just minutes later, when he'd returned, he was surprised to see the two plain-clothed policemen already pulling up on the verge at the bottom end of the grove. The old man, waving his arms and bawling as loud as he could, finally gained their attention.

Detective Sergeant Antonio Bellini pulled back the field-hand's leather tunic and recoiled at the sickening sight of *Signor* Ashton's barely recognisable body. 'Well, it seems you were right, sir.'

Detective Inspector Allessandro Leopardi stared down at the body with as much repulsion. Less than an hour ago it had been his solemn duty to arrest this man, believing him to be a determining factor in the death of the millionaire's son. But he held no grudge towards the deceased whose body now lay smashed almost beyond recognition. Slowly shaking his head with much regret, he spoke to the corpse plaintively. 'I should have listened to you my friend and for that I'm truly sorry.'

The sergeant hadn't grasped the meaning of the inspector's remark but asked, 'But how did you know it was the Englishman?'

The inspector felt compelled to ignore his colleague's question for he didn't really know the answer. When they heard the ambulance and the other police cars rapidly approaching up through the hollow village, the sergeant asked, 'Which of us is going to inform his wife?'

'You'd better leave that to me,' the inspector replied. 'Never in all my days has my judgement been so impaired,' he added, again slowly shaking his head in remorse.

The sergeant was lost, 'I don't quite follow you, sir.'

'Well don't you see Bellini; our English friend here has finally succeeded in putting an end to his own tortured mind. And although he was probably unaware of it himself, I think this is what he had been trying to tell us.'

Following a pause for reflection, the sergeant asked, 'Do you still think he had something to do with the young man's death, sir?'

'Oh, undoubtedly... but that's now something I'm afraid we'll never be able to prove.'

THE END

Acknowledgements

A gain, I would like to express my gratitude to my good friend and editor, James Essinger, for his ongoing guidance, proficiency and above all, his patience. My deepest thanks also to my dear friends, Sarah Heathfield for her invaluable assistance with the manuscript, Christine Melloy for her help with the correspondence, and also Charlotte Mouncey for the cover design and the typesetting.

And of course, my heartfelt thanks to my wonderful wife Judy, without whose continued support and encouragement this book wouldn't have been possible.

Finally, may I also extend my best wishes to all the inspirational and lovely people Judy and I met in Malcesine, Lake Garda.